Everybody Knows

What T⧗me It Is

But Nobody Can Stop the Clock

By Reginald Martin

PRESS

Printed in the USA

Library of Congress Control Number: 2009940208

Martin, Reginald

Everybody Knows What Time it is

ISBN 10: 1-60801-011-2
ISBN 13: 978-1-60801-011-0
Copyright © 2010 by UNO Press
All rights reserved.

UNOPRESS

THE ENGAGED WRITERS SERIES
University of New Orleans Publishing
Managing Editor, Bill Lavender
http://unopress.uno.edu

Engaged Writers Series Board:
Peter Thompson, Roger Williams University
Jerry Ward, Dillard University
Cynthia Hogue, Arizona State University
Réda Bensmaïa, Brown University
Donald Wellman, Daniel Webster College
Christopher Burawa, Austin Peay State University
Adam Braver, Roger Williams University
Brenda Marie Osbey, Louisiana State University

For: PHW, K., and Dexter Wayne Pierce

Everybody Knows

What T⧖me It Is

But Nobody Can Stop the Clock

"History, n. An account mostly false, of events mostly unimportant, which are brought about by rulers mostly knaves, and soldiers mostly fools."
— Ambrose Bierce, *The Devil's Dictionary*

🗙

"History, if done the way it's always been done, makes pretty readable fiction."
— R. Martin, *Non-Fiction-Fiction*

🗙

"… I didn't mean to take up all your sweet time./ I'll give it back to you one of these days."
— Jimi Hendrix, "Voodoo Chile"

Chapter 1

"*More than anyone else, the journey was necessary for me. I mean, it was for my own self, or else there wouldna been no me— at least no me I woulda wanted to recognize once I didn't go.*"

Zip looked up from his lover's desk in the near future, perspiration beading on his face and arms, speaking with Afro-inflections in a self-signifying attempt to reassure himself that the way he'd spent the last three years of his life had not ruined the remaining years he had left. July is despairingly hot in Memphis, yet he had purposely turned off his lover's central air in the recently transfigured cotton warehouse, opening the window and pushing the ridiculously expensive, rented, mahogany desk out onto the concrete and steel balcony, away from its two-bedroom, purple lushness, and began writing on it— the first time he had ever used it for that purpose— sitting completely nude, facing the southeast.

To his right, the setting sun glared from across the River onto enormous condo-towers of brown, mirrored glass, which rose, and, thankfully, blocked out almost completely the slum row houses to the north, except for the backporch of one of them, on which stood a brown baby, its bare body sweating and its face effortlessly pushed into an overwhelming smile as it stared without squinting into the glaring purple sun.

Zip used his right hand as a squeegee, pushing sweat from his almost hairless chest all the way to his groin and whisking it to his right and into the air with a flick. In his left hand, his glass of club soda with an entire lime, whose end he had cut off, condensated, dropping cool beads of water onto his bare left leg. He dried his other hand in his black, short, curly hair, which he had only now decided to grow into the longest dreadlocks he could muster to manifest RAS-I Peters, and pushed the seven or eight hundred pages of his manuscript into one pile. He looked down at the fifth page of **Chapter 1** (later to be cut in the Bantam edition [later owned by an Australian toilet paper conglomerate]) as the-character-that-was-he explained to another elderly winner in the old folks country-club home an epiphany that had once over-taken him.

"*See, umon tell you what your problem is. You want the REAL TRUTH, and you a damn fool if you think um gon give anybody that… except her. That's just like you Fans who been rich all your life. You want a little realism to convince yourself you not a mannequin. But I will tell you when I met her… how I met her… her.*

I was in that phase that comes right after or right before a big decision in your life— the crossroads y'know… and you feel you haveta make a move because the decisions you made before didn't work out and all of a sudden you realize that one day The Three Stooges are gonna come over the satellite, but you ain't gon be able to seeum. But they're gonna go right on anyway, slapping each other with pies and drinking paint, and even your memories ofem will be gone.

"It's that phase um talkin about man, right in there for most people after they give up too soon on romance and finally get off the caine, and just before they find Jesus in some alley or some public bathroom in a blinding light and start blabbering over the monitor about how great they are now cause they ain't of this world no more and ain't like your dumb-ass no more—it was right in there dude, when I mighta fell over the edge like those like-humans, that I met her. And meeting her made me change myself back into what I was before I got to that edge… um tellin you dude, there ain't never been nobody more filled with seriousity."

* * *

As he looked back away from his manuscript, he could see, hear, and smell directly in front and below, the broad expanse of powerful, brown water rushing past in its journey from Minneapolis to New Orleans.

"NewOrleansNewOrleans," Zip mumbled over and over until it became a refrain. *"That water is walkin to New Orleans."*

A tear mingled with sweat rolled down his face, hanging for a second from his wet, perfectly etched black beard, and then fell through the perforation of the balcony grating to land four stories down on a slender, dark-brown, immaculately manicured hand with still-fresh thorn scratches that reached for the buzzer with the words

"S E I D A H J A C K S O N Suite - 51556"

expertly and personally labeled beneath it.

"I shouldna kissed her," Zip whispered into the glare of the setting sun, *"I should just have let Sleeping Beauty sleep."*

In the noise of the urban dusk, all was poised and silent, like a panther on the point of springing. As he slowly rotated his head to the southeast to acknowledge the buzzer, in the Delta dusk there was a hope and a future as perfect as the sun going down.

* * *

In late July of an earlier year, Zip looked up from his CRT at Sparkling Inns and said, loudly enough for the other workers in his four-seated, plastic, "urban-ready" carpeted, wall-sectioned cubicle to hear: "What in the fuck am I doing here?"

The reservations division of Sparkling Inns was 99% female, and the girls in Zip's section loved it when he had these intermittent expulsions of Afro-American angst during the 4:30 p.m. - 1 a.m. shift.

"I know that's right! You tellem Zip honey. I got a asshole on the line who says his toilet— in Atlanta right— was stopped up, and when he pushed the flusher it blew up and shot shit all over him and his kids." Marilyn howled, bending over with laughter in her unsitable chair. Reservationists were not allowed to stand; it was "unprofessional."

"He wants to know what I'm going to do about it. I told him he should call the desk right, and he says, 'They're all asleep. Nobody answers.'"

Marilyn continued holding her forefinger over the mouthpiece to her headset.

"So I says, 'Well sir, what can I do about it? I'm in Memphis right.' And he says, 'You can start out by coming down here and licking this shit off me and my kids. You fuckers made this reservation— and this hotel is in the nigger part of Atlanta I might add— and you're on the TV all the time talkin about 'Super Service.' I figure the least you can do is come down here and service me.' Oh he's wild!"

"Guess you didn't have your black voice turned on and he couldn't tell. Ask him where there ain't no niggers in Atlanta," said Debra, leaning back in her chair from her terminal.

"Yea, tell him to go out in the street and tell somebody out there to service him. Them niggers'll clean that shit off his ass real fast," Zip snarled.

"Yea, yea, you talk to him Zip. Tell the motherfucker off." Marilyn removed her headset and held it toward Zip.

"Yea, talk that talk to him, Zip!" said Vickie, just picking up on what was rather a routine occurrence on a Friday night in reservations.

On Friday nights, guests wanted shit licked off them, called up on

December 31 at 11 p.m. and wanted to be given complimentary rooms with a view in the middle of beachfront Miami for the midnight celebration; the guests also wanted the reservationist to jack off while the guests did the same during the reservation call. And then they wanted a male reservationist to video the masturbating females— on DVD-R— and send them a copy, complimentary, of course.

On Friday nights, televisions "accidentally" fell from 10-story windows onto the fat bellies of visiting shoe-salesmen drunk in the pool, and it was the reservationists' fault. On Friday nights, peoploids called from Conway, Arkansas and asked questions like, "If I push my two single beds together, does reservations have a sheet the right size to cover the two beds?" From Des Moines, Iowa they wanted to know if reservations would protect them from Satan, who they were sure was in the spare-tire holder of their Winnebago at that very moment. From Tulsa, Oklahoma they wanted to know would reservations provide them with a loaded-gun for protection if they took a room with an adjoining door. There were marriage proposals, threats of patricide, long-winded explanations on the subtleties between 100 different species of trout, and requests for condoms and hair-relaxer on Friday nights. One woman had even called up one Friday night and told a reservationist she was going to blow up the reservations center in Memphis because she'd gotten pregnant by her fat, ugly boyfriend in a room reservations had reserved for them.

Zip pushed the headset away.

"Nah, I ain't got shit to say to his sorry ass. He's got enough problems. Funky motherfucker."

"Awww Zip, come on baby. It's Friday night," said Marilyn. "We need some fun. We gotta work here til everything's closed. Dry-ass Memphis. Might as well be livin west of the River, which is a death worse than fate let me tell you."

"Naaa, I ain't got nothing to say. What am I doing here?" Zip asked himself again, standing and looking out the window at the parking lot.

"I make $18,000 a year. If I work here another ten years, I'll make a whole $20,000. Let's see, $18,000 a year entitles me to a small Japanese car," (though his large car payments went for something more… traditional), the mortgage on the two rooms he'd added to his parents' home, groceries, two insurances and a night out once a month. "I can carry two furniture payments, and if I work here a hundred fuckin years, I ain't never gonna get ahead enough to get up a down payment for a decent house in a decent neighborhood with the other stuff I need.

"This is not even takin into consideration all the years I'm losin off my life undergoin this constant CS: Caucasian Stress. Caucasians are strange beings— especially the black ones— who think the world should always be made over, not in their image, but in the image they think they possess. But I'm supposed to be glad I got this mindless job, right? It's like being in the fuckin Twilight Zone. I expect Rod Serling to jump up outta the CRT and say, 'Submitted for your approval, Joe Negro, an existential cog in the vast Caucasian Corporate System, unhappy with his fiscal and social lot. Tonight he will do something… different.'"

"Ooo Zip! Talk that talk honey. You so crazy!" screamed Marilyn.

"Marilyn, shut up! See, yall been conditioned. They been keepin you either outta work or workin at piss-ass jobs for so long yall happy to get any job where you don't have to wear onea them clown suits and push Jolly Snacks. Me, I ain't meant for this shit um tellin you. The owners of this joint know all about us cause they know that if human beings work for a system long enough, to those human beings that system will become more important than the human beings who make the system work."

The girls all started to smile and put their index fingers over their mouth-pieces, ignoring the calls. They knew what was coming, and it felt like a good one.

"Now, the system makes your lives wretched, but you hate yourselves and your own wretchedness, *never* the system that makes you into things rather than human beings. Hating the ISM is too big for you, over your dumb-ass heads. Jesus will swoop down from heaven any minute and save you. He'll make all the bad people read American Colonial literature, and He'll pay the health insurance of all the good people like yourselves.

"The system becomes the only thing that works right in your miserable lives, and if something goes wrong with the system, it must be your fault, right, never the fault of the system. Look, I'm 30 years old and it's 2017. Now can any of yall tell me how Ernest Falwell got promoted supervisor over me? I been here two years with 'no blemishes' on my record as they say, and that sucker has been here 6 months and he's in the bathroom every break snortin up everything— face bowls, floor tiles, toilets, everything— and now he's a supervisor. Can yall explain that to me?"

"Shhh. Shut up and sit down now Zip," whispered Debra, "you gittin too loud. You know he's white and loves Jesus. Ain't that enough? Anyway, they said you didn't have no intra-personal skills."

"Yea, I lack the intra-personal skills alright— it oughta be 'inter-personal' by the way— but um justa nigger, don't know no English. Lord knows I don't know how to communicate with people and that freaked-out, Southern Baptist, coke-head who can't pronounce the word *skill* without adding enough short I's to choke a Clydesdale does. But hey, that's alright. Here's some intra-personal skill for their asses." Zip exploded a deafening fart across the cubicle. The smell was like a living thing.

"Oooweee! Zip you nasty. You foul boy. You smell like you dead. Don't be punishin us for they sins. Oooweee!" yelled Vickie.

All the girls stood up, fanning with their hands, as Zip balled up and fell to the floor convulsing in ropes of laughter. Zip jerked his headset out of the terminal and looked up at the girls who were still fanning.

"Why don't yall let me show you some of my intra-personal skills? You be the judge. 'Does he or doesn't he have the adequate intra-personal skills to advance in a sterling corporate system like this one? Only coke-headed white men know for sure.'" He let out a resounding barrage of farts which took on discreet identities of their own.

Debra said, "Zip will you please cut that shit out? Down there foddin like that. A grown man. Really!"

"I'm through fartin around," said Zip. His thoughts came out in a long ream of compound and periodic sentences, and he punctuated the end of each with machine-gun-like little pellet-farts.

"I'm through fartin around and I'm through eatin shit and yall can stay here if you want to **(BUURRT!)**. When you wake up you'll be 55 and they'll be kickin your asses out the door to keep from payin your health insurance **(BRRRUWUWUWU!)**. And with what you've saved over the years maybe you can afford a .25 to blow your stressed-out brains onto the rest-home floor **(HOOOEEEEEEBRRRTTT!)**."

The girls looked at each other. They weren't laughing anymore and neither was Zip. But he was standing now and still shouting.

"I mean, don't chall see what's happnin? Don't chall wanna do nothin with your lives? Don't chall wanna do no more than make your pennies, eat, and get high? Don't you ever wonder why everything is so messed up? I mean, there's gotta be somewhere where black people ain't the shit of the earth … surely. Well, this is it for my ass. Um clockin out permanently. And um gettin as far away as I can from this corporate cocksucker and backwardsass Memphis. Niggers in Memphis paid library taxes to build a new library and couldn't even go in the damn library. That's it, um through. Um scit-scat-

long-gone-look-for-me-again-when-you-see-me-comin outta this mother!"
He put his headset in its packet and started for the supervisor's office.

"Where you goin Zip, back to Africa?" Marilyn said as a joke, trying
to get him to relax, but she saw that he was through, and she missed him
already.

"Nah, um goin to Atlanta. At least there toilets blow up on Friday night.
I mean, maybe the toilet just got tired of being shit in, and he said, 'Hey, let
me give you a little of this back and see how you gon like it.' I mean, did you
ever think of that? Umon miss yall." Marilyn bent down to her terminal to
take a call.

"Hello, Sparkling Inns reservations, Marilyn speaking. What city and
state are you requesting please?" The male voice responded:

"Honey, I wanna go to the land of pussy and honey. Do you know where
that is? You think you got enough room for me?"

She clicked him off immediately. She was in no mood. When she stood
back up and looked through the supervisor's window, Zip was gone.

* * *

Aerobics classes in New Orleans in July are something different, even for
the jaundiced and cynical among the IN-SHAPE of the urban crowd. There
has from time to time been a placating rumor covertly circulated that there
are places on earth more humid than New Orleans. There were whispers
about Calcutta, Kuala Lumpur, Kinshasa, and certain places in the Brazilian
interior; places where it was said inhabitants had to hold pitchers of water to
their mouths during the entire day-light period because sweat oozed out of
them as rapidly as they imbibed liquids; places where the national mascot
was a 27,000 BTU Carrier Air Conditioning unit which was worshipped as
an icon.

But looking out of the condensated windows that faced Gravier Street
as she alternately popped up from her lower back stretches, Siedah Jackson
doubted that such rumors were true. Everyone in the converted receiving
warehouse, whose owner had had the Draconian idea of leaving the original,
massive ceiling fans and not adding central air ("For the atmosphere of
the place" he would say a year later, just before being sent to Joliet prison
convicted on a half-baked scam to add PCP to his grandmother's patented
Gumbo recipe and market it as *Extra Spicy Hoodoo Jumbo Gumbo*), stood
in their own personal puddles of sweat, wondering why humans voluntarily

paid someone to put them through the torture of impossible muscular contortions for 30 minutes in a city where the blink of an eye made you sweat so much you had to have a change of clothes.

And anyway, the men in formation behind Siedah didn't need to work-out to sweat. In a blinding blizzard in the middle of January in Nome, Alaska, Alluits naked for a swim would have sweated at the sight of Siedah. Six feet of mobile ebon elegance with the cool reserve of Sarah Vaughn in Piedmont Park on a Sunday in May, Siedah stretched at the waist to the left, and then to the right. God had not only taken his time when he made Siedah, he had encoded on her hard disc a program which could not be duplicated. She was at least 100 gigabytes of serious dynamite. And although Ms. Greer thought she was leading the class, she was only titular; its true Pharaoh was the obsidite princess in a purple Spandex body-suit who even had the women in the class following her lead; the men had long ago ceased paying any attention to Ms. Greer and moved and breathed and sweated in rhythm only with Siedah.

And though the others could not see it in the eyes of she who stared out the window, there was a longing inside of her that was as deep and as thick as the condensated swelter she could see rising above Lake Ponchartrain.

Life is a funny thang ain't it? Funny. She had thought winning an acting scholarship to Xavier was a step in the right direction. Then, later, her changing to an engineering major and graduating at the head of her class from Tulane seemed a big deal. An accomplishment. Then that job at NEGCO and $80,000 a year, and then the Charles White prints on the wall and the Elizabeth Catlett fist figurine on the cocktail table seemed enough, and it seemed that there would finally be an end of that awful period in her life labeled as "PRE-." The hoops would be jumped through. The degrees finished. Respect granted. THE MONEY IN THE BANK. She could get on with the serious business of living and loving. Ha! But there was no stasis. The lioness jumped through one hoop only to see an endless line of them in front of her, with a last one only dimly sensed, not even seen, behind which immediately lay DEATH. Simultaneously, her past lay just behind her like clothes shed in a dawn run to the Gulf, and the future extended liquidly, coolingly, but before she could immerse herself, it receded before her touch, leaving more hoops on the beach, stuck in the sand of the present.

First of all, she had found that 80 grand a year was nothing these days—especially for a person with tastes like hers. Educated tastes. Well-read tastes. A woman with a brain as sharp as her fingernails, who knew the difference between a reel-to-reel and a CD, a fox and a chinchilla, a Porsche and a Ferrari, and Hemingway and Samuel Delany, and wanted only the best.

Also, she was beginning to feel unstuck in a world which ran only on luck, timing, and money. While her material interests pushed her to distraction trying to figure out ways to get more, she was enough of her father's daughter to know that capital had to have something else to go along with it to make its luxury worth enjoying. She didn't *need* anything from any man. But what she wanted was to be in love with one.

However, she was also in tune with her own time and her own experiences enough to know that having sex with men was one thing, but loving them was like learning hieroglyphic astrophysics backwards in Martian on LSD. Loving men was a whole nother thing altogether. Anyone with sight could look at her and tell she hadn't hurt for male attention. She still balled up in laughter when she remembered that guy who ran into the back of a garbage truck while he was watching her jog down Gravier one day. No, the affairs had been great, but she'd decided long ago that sex— even great sex as she had occasionally had from time to time from those guys who didn't drop the ball— was 180 degrees different than love. Sex was taken for granted and a constant. Love was something for which she had never made time.

She'd seen love for men make the women she went to college with stand on dorm ledges at 2 a.m. and scream for Jesus as an escort, cause they were coming His way anyway. She'd seen love turn 4.0's into morons. She'd seen love convince a woman, who couldn't even support herself, to have babies she didn't want, to get a man who didn't want her or the babies. She'd seen LOVE do all these things and she stayed as far away from it as she could. LOVE was like an airborne virus. If you didn't cover every orifice, the shit would blow into some hole and you'd be dead in three days—or worse, you'd live a long time remembering what love was and that it is what you can no longer have.

Siedah had had goals that had to be reached for the life of her own self-concept. And she had counted herself as lucky: she was a woman who loved making love, and who could have an orgasm without attributing it to a divine act. She had a good time, and if they wanted to dissipate in the humidity after-the-fact, that was fine with her. But, you know, nobody ever evaporated on Siedah. They clung to her like sweat until she had to flick them off.

And she'd had it with these terrestrial cowards who used fuel-injected insecurities to power their own selfishness. Always running around the dance clubs talking about they didn't believe in reason. "I don't believe in reason," they'd say, "let's just go with the flow" cause believing in reason would force them to make *cold, hard* choices about how responsible they were gonna be for the outcome of their own lives. Yea, the motherfuckers didn't believe in reason, but their reason made them "forget" the Ramses and leave them in the glove compartment, "forget" to take their pills, made them forget your birthdays and your anniversaries. Naw, these 21st-century boys and girls didn't believe in reason, but their reason would make them get up at 2 a.m. while you were sleeping and eat the very last Danish out of the refrigerator, and then crawl back in the bed with you without the common civility to wipe the crumbs of the crime from their luscious lips.

But now she was ready for something else. Yeah, a dual-dimensional dude who had those quirks that made you wash every milliliter of your sexy self when you knew he was comin over, cause there was no tellin *what* he'd put his mouth on the minute he walked through the door, and who also knew without you having to tell him to go get the wet, warm towel and press it down on your lower tummy when it was that time and not other times.

Good relationships are such a matter of blind-luck timing; now she was ready, and nobody was around. It made you wonder why anybody tried to "plan" relationships or "do the right things," cause none of that stuff seemed to matter in the end.

> *It's a number 9/*
> *And I ain't got time/*
> *to worry bout nothin/*
> *but what I ain't already got.*

Kicking in time with the drums and bass, stopping only to grind to the synthesizer, she realized it was not going to be easy. For Siedah, the man had to be something brand new. God would have to encode him, too.

> *The world spinnin all around/*
> *Like life in a trance.*
> *But it don't bother me.*
> *Cause I know how to dance.*

Shit, if she had to, she'd make him herself. She'd sweat it out.

Chapter 2

"**W**hat is it that I want anyway?" Zip thought to himself. "I got myself a good, average life here. Hell, it's better than every other black guy's life I know my age. I got a job— a boring, pain-in-the-ass job— but it's a job. 18 G's a year. I stay with my folks, and they buy all the groceries and pay the utilities. I got the fastest, sleekest car in the world; I love zippin through them angry Negro streets at dawn, and I got 6 or 7 women other guys would sell their houses to go out with. I got no kinda V.D., no kids so I avoid that automatically court-deducted $369 a month. And I know um beautiful cause I look like my mama. So what's the problem? I mean, you know, what's the deal?"

Zip unlocked the door to his part of his parents' house. He lived in the back in a three-room addition, which was "all a bachelor needed," he'd told himself while signing the loan papers. Now, it somehow seemed very stark, even though it was filled with every technological pleasure device known— and some not known until Zip had built them.

He was good at adding little stuff to things which already existed. That is, he was good at additions, until it came to adding the right catalyst to make his life move in the right direction. There was a problem now existing in his life— in fact the state of his life was his problem— and he didn't know how the problem started, so he had a hard time trying to add or subtract something to make things right.

With most LIFEAL problems, you can see right away that there's absolutely nothing you can do: the latest supremist talked all day about "preserving the peace" by beating children with night-sticks, tear-gassing women, bull-dozing tin-roofed houses, and rewriting various parts of their particular holy book, and there was nothing you could do. You watched your cousin around the corner go to the penal farm for ten years with hard labor for receiving a stolen $180 television and then flipped the channel to see Made-OFF walking out of the courthouse,—smiling— knowing he would not live for ten years. Politicians would start wars with their banker friends, leave office, and the newest puppet-in-charge would not allow his old friends to be prosecuted for war crimes. Every channel on the TV was filled with the sexual predilections of some sports god, while no one could find in 999 channels the death toll that day from the illegal wars or a fair discussion of what was about to happen in a closed-door meeting in Copenhagen. And there was nothing you could do. Noticed that all of the old Confederacy states of the south—your home—the one *you* built— shrewdly took the Stars and Bars from the old flag and shrunkem down, twistedem, puttem in circles, or stuckem in the corner, so that while it *wasn't* the flag they were ordered to destroy (you know, the ones they used to wave at the U. of Mississippi football games with their half squads of black players ["Hell no *they* ain't fergittin"]), it *was* still the same flag that the losers were ordered to destroy, and there was nothing you could do. Watched as the boy in the white jacket with the stethoscope around his neck told the 89-year-old black maid—who raised him and wiped his snot and his ass when he was only an accident his parents didn't have time to deal with—watched him tell her that he "really would like" to do a double mastectomy on her and increase the length and quality of her life. Nothing you could do. And freaked in anguish cause the Coyote *NEVER* got to rend, tear, and eat that goddamed Roadrunner. There was simply nothing you could do to change these things, so you pushed them to the back of your mind in an encrypted file that even you didn't know the code to get back into.

But then there were those LIFEAL things that you thought maybe you could do something about if you could only figure out what to change, what to add or subtract that would straighten the whole mess out and make your life like June and Ward's: perfect in every way. To those kinds of problems in his urban world, Zip thought he already knew what to add or subtract:

He owned one 15' satellite dish, one Sony Big Screen HD TV in an oriental cabinet with digital tuning, teletext, 378 direct access channels and two picture-in-picture features, two Sony 35" HD video monitors with 1200 x 1500 lines of resolution plus on-screen programming, MTS stereo and 20 other on-screen menu displays, three Sony color HD TVs with sleep-function timers, two In-Focus HD projectors with 16:9 screens, three Sony 700 watt HD receivers with 12 video/audio inputs each, three Bang and Oulfson 95-watt-per-channel ETCs, two Sony Dual Blu-ray DVD recorders, one Sony 8" reel-to-reel recorder he'd bought off E-bay, two Sony AM-FM clock radios (whose built-in hard drives automatically made the sound of Minnie Ripperton hitting the high note in "Loving You" to awaken him each morning), 5,000 home-made DVDs, with the predominant number containing recordings of music videos, the '04, '08, '12, and '16 Olympics, and Charlie Chan movies, 1,500 classic vinyl albums, 5,000 CDS, most of them of post-contemporary jazz, a synclavier he had "appropriated" from the Niemann Marcus shopping train parked down by the river, and 1,500 mini-DVDs, almost every one of them soul or R&B/funk/fusion recordings, except the Laurie Anderson and Mahalia Jackson tapes, which he kept around for creative inspiration.

He had the late **DONNEL JONES** (pronounced **DUN-L**) on CD, reel-to-reel, mini-CD, and the new audio DVD, cause it was **DONNEL**. On his desk was a 3-D Holo-Screen, 100 gigs of RAM, with an external disc-drive of 1500 gigabytes holding seven different DTP packages that interfaced with his $5,000 sound-to-notes music package, two Hewlett-Packard Laser Jet+10 color graphic-based printers, one Canon LaserJet printer which doubled as a color scanner, and one dot-matrix printer (cause he worshipped history and some anachronisms), all of which interfaced with his netbook he had super-glued into his red, black, and green briefcase. When he couldn't watch, listen, or read, he wrote on his three large desks, all together roughly one quarter as large as his id, pushed together and filling his office, so that he had to crawl under them to get to the computer or crawl over the top of them to get to the bathroom. And what he wrote was autobiography turned into fantasy. Or was it the other way around?

And speakers.

Zip owned eight Matthew Polk SDA SRS Speakers, with four woofers, mid-ranges, and tweeters each, which he had distributed evenly, putting four in his den and four in his bedroom; one per corner in each room. All of these were enhanced by special amplifier Boom Boxes Zip had made. In the bathroom were four Sony bookshelf speakers connected to a $2,300 portable Sony Jam Box, which weighed 137 pounds. The B&O speaker system he kept near his bed to drown out intimate moments from his parents.

He was, obviously, a man of his time.

This fact was attested to not only by the techno-representation of art in his three rooms, but also by his over-extended credit, which did not allow for even a candy bar after the 1st of each month. As far as he could tell, every penny of his 18 G's for the next three years was to be sent to Visa. Like so many people of the early 21st-century, he knew there was no such thing as a future— especially an economic future— for people at his income level, so he made the future now.

But his techno-stuff left him cold this night. He was headed for the possessions that really mattered to him, kept him alive: his massive collection of books.

He flipped on the lamp that sat on a line of his books. At last count, Zip owned 5,700 paper-backs and 3,000 hard-covers. This was not counting the stacks and stacks of photo-copied books he owned, having violated every existing copyright known to anyone whenever there was a sale on copies. He'd stand at the Kodak copier for hours, getting 350 page hard-cover, first editions for $2.75.

Tonight he was not gentle with his gargantuan pile of Western thought— "Mostly the kinda bullshit that keeps poor people poor"— Zip had often said about all the writing he had read, but he read voraciously, a book every two days, anyway.

Throwing tomes in the air, he growled, "Where is that asshole Nietzsche? NietzcheNietzcheNietzsche! Sounds like a grasshopper rubbing his hind-legs just before he spits."

"There you are you manic-depressive, German Mensch you. Running around Munich talking about you a Superman and shit and dyin of the clap you got from a 2 Mark an hour ho. A great Western philosopher you is. I wouldn't take a whole gross of you for one Toni Morrison.

"Let's see now, what was that I was reading from old Freddy the other night? LesseeLessee. Chapt. 12, yeah, 'Existential Angst.' That's what buggin my ass! I got me some authentic, Afro-American angst crawling up my spine. Let me see if old Fred put a cure in here… Naw! That's what I hate about philosophers. Always pointin out problems but never doing nothing to help nobody. 'I got my ass outta angst; you get your own ass out.' And Fred you of all people, sittin in Berlin blabbering syphilitic idiocy while the Nazis stole your theories to use for UberMann lies; wipin out whole populations. Philosophers! None ofem fit to tie the shoelaces of a man like Dr. King— except maybe Camus, who whadn't no German. Obviously, umon have to solve this problem my damn self, and I don't know no other way than to get the hell outta Dodge. I got to move to groove."

He flopped down on a stack of papers and books, his anus pressing hard in divine symmetry with Blake's *Milton* and his scrotum drooping onto Greenlee's *The Spook Who Sat By the Door*.

"Zip! Zippyeeeeeee! Honey you gon eat or what? Roast and spaghetti with a lotta hoop cheese. Zip, Zip you in there or what?"

"Yeah, mama, um comin. I'll be right there."

He hadn't thought about tellin his parents he was gonna leave— goin to no job— and leaving in the Camaro in search of some kinda… something.

That would be hard. Especially leaving his mother. She had always been the receiver for his wavelength, and now he was gonna sign off without so much as a group of call-letters.

Zip's father and mother waited until he got to the table to say grace. Even though Zip believed only in what he could see (and he was spiritually suspicious of that), he had always gone along with his parents' religious practices, because, first, he knew that logic is a dead-end anyway; you end up materially and substantially proving that everything is anti-human and that you're just some rich boy's toilet cover, and that when you're no more good, you get flushed; in other words, you pointed out the obvious. Then you ended up like that fool Nietzsche, sittin up in the asylum playing with yourself.

That the world was awful was old news. The hard part and the important thing was to figure out how to make scads of money and not be distracted or depressed from making money by "THE FACTS." And secondly, his parents were the two kindest and most caring people he had ever known. No point in starting a lotta stuff. You could never win with what you saw as your parents' short-comings; you could only hurt their feelings.

"Let us bow our heads." His father, a retired janitor and another insatiable reader, always led grace.

"Holy Father, we ask in your son's Jesus' name to bless this table, and we thank you for havin the whole family here at the table once again. Amen."

* * *

Whenever all the praying or moaning or singing started, Zip's bicameral brain went through equal mitosis: two halves split from one original and formed a left and a right, completely opposed in thought procedure, reason, and beliefs. The left side of this split-pea was easy to understand, linear, rational, and the side with which Zip found himself in easiest agreement. It hummed out thoughts like these:

"Why is my father sitting there now embarrassing himself? He knows as well as I do that he is throwing all those eloquent words into emptiness. Sitting there praying. He, of all people, should know better.

"Didn't he tell me that they used to have those big church services out in the country and they'd rock and pray... but nothing ever got any better. God, how did he describ'em?

"First there would be no one in the church except the pianist, and he would sit down all prim and proper and smile at the ushers, and it would be like 10:59 a.m., and then he would make his back straight and open his mouth just slightly and he would hit a middle C, and the ushers would open the doors and tell the people they'd better come on in then.

"And then when everyone was seated, the pianist would strike up the first chord of "Peace, Be Still!" and the two side doors adjacent to the baptistry would open up and the choir would file in from both sides simultaneously, the altos and the tenors from the right, and the sopranos and the bass singers from the left, and then they would meet in the middle like two waves and crest and slosh back to fill out both sides of the choir stand.

"And in the middle of the song, the minister and assistant ministers would come out and everybody in the sanctuary would rise and the minister would speak the words loudly that the choir was repeating more slowly, a different beauty, behind him, and everyone would hear the words from the preacher but sing them with the choir:

> *'The winds and the waves shall obey My will.*
> *PEACE! Be Still!*
> *PEACE! Be Still!*
> *And whether the wrath of the storm-tossed sea,*
> *or winds, or waves or what'er may be,*
> *No power can disrupt the Master's plan,*
> *the Ruler of sea and sky and land.'*

"And then the preacher would tell the congregation to sit and they would.

"Then from the last swivel chair on the raised platform that rose in front of the pulpit, a voice would come from—it seemed—somewhere so deep in Mississippi that it crooned more from Mozambique than the blackest state in the Union, and the prim pianist would know that if he touched one key on that third-hand, battered, de-tuned piano, everybody in the joint would give him the eye.

"And Deacon Susanberry would continue to sing from a time that half the people in the church couldn't remember, but a time that no one in the church could forget, a time that knew only the human throat as an instrument in an alien land:

Susanberry: *'I heard the voice of Jesus say—'*

Choir and Congregation (CC):
CC: `I-I-I
H e-e-e-ard
The V-o-o-o-ce o-o-of
J-E-E-E-SUS S-A-A-A-Y—"
S: *Come unto to Me and rest*
CCC: C-o-o-o-me un-n-nto
M-e-e-e a-a-a-and
Rest—'

"And that tune evoking that time when those slaves in St. Augustine, Savannah, Starksville, Selma, and Sommerville adopted a religion and syncretized Christianity into something useful—the only thing that they could use to survive and propagate, to hang on until the early 20th century in that church that day where the older ones among them knew they were about to amalgamate into the Cathedral of the Self. And the younger ones, including pop, watched and trembled at the power of a people who had no power.

"And when that exchange was done, for all of those people to feel as one spiritual body united by a song composed in misery in movement toward something, anything, more better…

"… to believe all that," Zip thought as his left brain continued to pretend to be impervious in its typical linear fashion, even as the right brain's erratic but incessant impulses easily seduced linearity into opening up to, hanging out with, and believing in the unseen, "how could anyone believe all that in such a… literal world? To believe in all that heaven when blacks continued to be made the perpetual Rodney Dangerfields of that rural landscape?"

"Jesus," Zip thought, "how can he sit there and embarrass the-part-of-me-that-is-he by doing that, and how did I turn out so oppositely undivided? Anybody can talk to me for five minutes and see that I know ain't nothin up in the sky but clouds. Hell, I don't even remember the details of all that old church stuff anyway."

* * *

As Zip looked up, his father was already picking up the roast to hand to his mother, and his mother was buttering bread for everybody.

He could see what they saw in each other, this former maid and former janitor, who had taught themselves to read and who had had a child so late in 1987 that even the black midwives thought the child would be strangely touched— if it lived. His father had refused to put his mother in the local hospital because the medical residents had said they'd better abort when his mother was only twelve weeks pregnant. "Too old," they said. And after all, she was only a black they were waiting on in the basement of the city hospital, only a few years after Brown broke the Board, and still fewer years since Memphis had even eliminated "Colored Day" at the Zoo. Their love was real because they sustained each other when their greatest fear was being only each other forever.

Thanks to the midwives, the child had lived. It *was* strange, and, for the first time, it didn't know what to say to two people with whom it had always effortlessly communicated on every topic— from (when he was 3) why his mother didn't stand and use her thing to pee like he did, to, when he was 13, discussing with his father the probability that nutrient deficiencies and stress were the sole causes of internal cancer— external to the millions of cases of industrially-caused cancers that nobody wanted to talk about. Zip swallowed his English peas, drank some of his iced-tea, cleared his throat, and started to speak. But his mother's eyes stopped him.

In his mother's eyes was everything, and everything to her was Zip. Her love for what he would become to her was always there, from the time she married his father when she was 16 and Lester was 19, to the time they finally gave up on producing any children— they had tried everything, and the wished-for "cures" had become more abominable than the reality they lived, and they flat quit all those "scientific" methods and simply enjoyed their formidable sex life, trying to give up the notion that a corporeal manifestation of their love which was more than the sum of them, but equal to their immense love for each other, would come of sex; trying to accept a fact of life which, in their minds, denied life.

Many more years would pass from the giving-up to the day Carrie would notice that she was putting on weight in a very odd fashion. She couldn't even speak when she came back from the mid-wife's house. One look at her face and Lester couldn't speak either. They both just sat in the kitchen, she in a cane-back chair and he on his knees between her thighs, crying and saying softly, softly, "Thank you."

And then there was Zip. Had his mother loved him any more, she would have loved him into another world where kids are kids forever and parents never grow old, but she wanted to keep him in this world, in this house, with her.

So it was then, when he looked across the table in late July and heard his mother say, "Yes, Zip honey, you got something to say? How was work today? Heah, eat some more corn. You gon grow up big like your daddy. And honey, let me tell you, this heah is a BIG man," rubbing Lester's thigh and winking, both Lester and Carrie bursting into laughter— when he looked into his mother's eyes, he knew it was going to be harder than a 16-year-old boy at a Halle Berry film festival to tell her he was going… somewhere to find… something, and he didn't know when he would be back.

"I'm sorry honey, I didn't mean to cut you off, but you know the devil gets in me and your daddy sometimes. Go head."

"Mama, um not gon grow up to be a big man. I'm already grown. I'm already a man. I been thinkin a lot lately, and I just… I been real dissatisfied y'know?" Zip spoke quietly, trying to figure out the right rhetoric for the situation. But there was no mode for saying goodbye.

"Something wrong at the job, son?" his father asked. "What?"

"Naw—yeah, well… everything. Um going nowhere, and they treat us like only Moe, Larry, and Curly deserve to be treated. By the time we hear about management openings on the reservations floor, some white boy done already put his name on the office door. But it's not just the racism funded by the economic set-up. It's that I can't do anything about it, and the other people I work with been without work for so long they glad— well, not glad, but their greatest fear is losing that little pleb job."

"Son," Lester put down his fork and knife and looked his son in the eyes, smiling, "You can always change jobs. Start looking now. If you feel like you can't stand it there another minute, quit. We'll tide you over until you find something."

"I don't want you to 'tide me over' off your savings and Social Security. I ain't made that way, and you of all people ought to know that cause you made me. Pop, um 30, and my next job is gon be the same lower-level entry for me. Some cracker in Shop Mart pants who can't speak a sentence— much less write one— telling me what to do. When I come up for promotion, if they let me stay that long, they'll tell me I lack the 'intra-personal-skills' for management and to wait. 'My day will come.' Well I don't want my damn day; they can keep it. But that's what I deserve for getting a degree in the things I love, English and Philosophy, and not loving the things I could have gotten degrees in, like BUSINESS. I ain't going through that shit no more. I gotta get outta that dead-end life with that dead-end bullshit. It takes too much energy to fight it, and I just ain't got the juice to spare.

"Besides, it's not just that, it's the way things are organized in companies that stifles and kills everybody. A lotta poor whites suffer at the bottom like we do; but they chalk it up to the 'workin life.' Well I ain't chalkin shit up so some lard-ass Fan can live off my work and send his kid to a school where the kid can get the right training for the right profession so she can make the right money to buy a house in the right neighborhood where she won't have to live with the wrong people who all look like me. That stinks. The whole thing stinks, and this is no news. Everybody knows what time it is, but nobody can stop the clock."

He had started to shout, which he had never done in their house before, much less in their presence, and he put his hands under his armpits to calm himself down and said very softly, "Um clockin out, before it's too late for me."

Carrie started to speak. "Son, let me tell you something. Wherever you go you gon be— "

"Wherever I go, mama," Zip cut in, "wherever I go mama, umon be me."

* * *

The moon was high out 3 nights later as Zip tied down onto the luggage rack of his car trunk his green, water-proof tarpaulin containing dishes, silver, a coffee-maker, and hangers. His parents gave him food and a thousand dollars, all they had set aside in a year, both of which he begrudgingly took as necessities. He had sold his techno-pleasure devices to pay off the outstanding balances on his many bills. His only bill now was the $350-per-month car note he was to mail to the National Bank of Commerce the first of every month for the next three years, which he had no idea how he would pay once his money ran out. Some day, some way, he would repay his parents, but he could never repay their love. The interest was too high. Money was a part of what he was driving off into the night to find, but the warmth that he hoped to find in Atlanta, he knew, could never equal what was exuding from his parents as they watched him check his tires.

"That right front looks a little low son. Better… check everything before you get on the highway." His father made no attempt to control his sense of loss.

His mother stood, hands clasped in front of her flowered dress, tears standing but not falling.

"You a different kind of man, Zip. The world's not ready for you … I love you—"

He hugged them both, let back the sunroof, and sat down behind the wheel.

"Mama, um sorry. I don't know what I'm going to, but every piece of my humanness and my blackness tells me I got to move." Zip turned the engine that whined as smooth as porcelain.

"You a new kind of man Zip," Lester forced out, and, then, remembering, "Not Greek, Not Jew, but a new race. You take care of… yourself."

* * *

I-40 heading east between Memphis and Nashville at mid-night is a black, black highway, with only white lines to demarcate safety and hazard.

Chapter 3

Nashville is Memphis minus the good music, the River, and a halfa million blacks; Nashville is to Memphis what Ripple is to Dom Perignon, what a FineMart suit is to a Gianni Versace, and what an inflatable doll is to Rhianna.

Not far from Nashville, the Snail Darter was being driven to extinction by corporate progress, and right down below the overpass of I-40, Nashville's other threatened species, the historically black brain factories of Tennessee State U., Fisk U., and Meharry Medical College, scraped for an existence in the shadows of the success of the Grand Ole Opry and Vanderbilt.

Back in '85 they put the new Japanese car plant in Smyrna, not far from Nashville, cause the word was that Memphis was fulla blacks and their sympathizers, and you know blacks love unions, the only things between them and Taiwan wages. The Japanese hated blacks for another easily understood reason too: the easiest way to define themselves as positive in the shadow of the Europeans was to define African-Americans as negative. It had always worked before. The poor and lower middle-class whites, who would make up the bulk of the work force out in Nowheresville, loved companies, it would seem, more than higher wages or grievance systems. At least that was the word.

"But you never can tell with blacks," Zip spoke aloud to himself, "they so paranoid."

He howled to himself as the last FingerDippin restaurant shrank in his rear-view mirror. He didn't have to come through Nashville in the first place— it was making the trip a quarter longer, actually— but the thought of taking the more direct alternative, a piecemeal, convoluted thruway of state highways, two-lane black tops, and country roads that would have taken him more or less straight across the bottom of the state from Memphis to Chattanooga, made him turn **Rhianna** up even louder and bound his stomach up into grandma's knots.

Every Southern black feared the un-urban Southern night, even at this late date. And it was odd how quickly black Americans had become synonymous with cities in every part of the country, after being almost totally a rural people up through the first decade of the 20th-century, as though, instinctively, they wanted nothing to do with anything that reminded them of plantations. So he drove through Nashville because he wanted to stay on the inter-state, something with mercury-vapor lights every 50 feet and Exxon stations with telephones every 5 miles or so. He wanted no Jimmy Hoffa-type mysteries concerning a late model Camaro with 100 CDS on the front seat and not a trace of a driver.

But that diminishing FingerDippin sign also meant there was that long, black incline to Chattanooga— an empty drive that would take him past such hot spots as Murfreesboro and Cookesville, then into the dim lights of Chattanooga. He turned the **Rhianna** louder to stave off that vertiginous and queasy feeling of plunging back into the bleakness of small-town America.

"Right, Right where you wanna be/
Is where you can be with me."

Synclavier.

* * *

About 30 miles out of Chattanooga you have to detour briefly through Alabama to get to Atlanta via interstate. Zip's heart raced, and then there was Georgia. 40 more minutes or so, and the Peachtree Plaza Tower and the Hyatt would be in sight. Ted Turner turf. WTBS and the Hawks. "The Best City in the Country" for professional black women, so *JET* magazine said anyway. And if it were in *JET*, hey, it must be a fact. Didn't they put Jackie Wilson's heart attack under the entertainment section? The beautiful hum of that Chinese V-1 and the silence of his shirt-pocket FuzzBuster allowed him to think about what he thought he might be searching for as he quietly moaned to Mart Inreg's "Asleep and Awake":

UM DRIVIN DOWN THESE CITY STREETS,"/
"Just couldn't stay in Memphis; distortin me, eatin me up. Wake up one day and you're the living dead. A SleepWalker.

"UM WIDE AWAKE BEHIND THE WHEEL,"/

"But I don't belong anywhere else but here. I *am* the fuckin South, everything it was, is, and wants to be.

"BUT I CAN'T SEE THE ROAD IN FRONT OF ME,"/

"Livin in our time is… damn near impossible. But giving up grates on my gonads so bad… so many people I know dead before 30, just goddamit gave up, rolled over.

"AND I JUST DON'T KNOW THE DEAL,"/

"I've seen with my own eyes all the sad stories live themselves, and read all them depressing black novels,

"SO I CRAWL TO THE COVERS,"/

"And I just can't live my life like that. Why don't those damn writers just blow my brains out with a .357 instead of torturing me for 500 pages or more? I just can't keep repeatin the same dull round generation after generation.

"NO DRUGS ALLOWED./
AND I TAKE MY ASS TO DREAMLAND,"

"Love myself first, which I already do too much; then, second, get the money now, for the future. Buy me some respect— or at least fear— from others.

"Money hopes all things, endures all things, bears all things, fulfills all things. Money never ends.

As for Affirmative Action programs, these shall fade away; as for living up to the spirit of the Constitution and the Declaration of Independence and the 1964-65 Civil Rights Acts, this, too, shall pass away. ERA will never be.

"When I was naive, I spoke like a damn fool, a SleepWalker. I acted like a damn fool, I reasoned like a damn fool. But after I read Camus and listened to Gil Scott-Heron, I gave up naive things.

"Though I hide behind and see through my Ray Bans darkly, when I meet the PERFECT face to face, the epiphany shall open my eyes, and money will pay for two 1st class seats to Jamaica.

"So youth, desire, energy, love, talent, luck, wisdom, beauty, and money abide, these nine, but the greatest of these is MONEY."

"WHERE THERE AIN'T NOBODY IN THE CROWD
BUT ME AND MY LADY SO FINE./
ITS THE BEST PLACE FOR ME
JUST CAN'T STAND BEING ASLEEP AND AWAKE AT THE SAME
TIME."

Repeating the last stanza again so his own rendition would bounce back into his ears over the hum of the Chinese engine, Zip smiled. He had everything he needed to figure out his life in the base of his throat.

* * *

On Bourbon Street in July, white female tourists from Texas hold dollar bills above the heads of short, graying black men who do flips and try to grab the dollars in their tumbling mouths. Not far from Pat O'Brien's is the bar in which Malcolm Cowley watched a youthful, drunken William Faulkner stand in the corner every night wearing no shoes and an enormous, but wearing flowing cape. Character manifests itself in New Orleans; it cannot be constrained.

As limber and as rustic as the aforementioned characters may be or may have been, Siedah was looking for a man of slightly higher character. If it had been sex only that she was looking for, things would have been much easier. And with the new exo-endorphin device (**EE!** for short) she'd bought at the local drug store, sex was more effortless— and more fun— than ever.

"When they're young, men are funny sexual creatures. This one over here wants you to keep your shoes on, that one over there wants to do it in the bathroom sink, this one here wants the two of you to sit on the top of the dresser in front of the mirror, and that one there wants peanut butter on his thing and wants you to lick it off— oops. That was my idea.

"Then by the time women get their bigger priorities outta the way at 35 or so— 2.3 kids, a mink, a big house and a career— and they're ready for the whipped cream and the ice cubes, the peanut butter and the "not-getting-out-of-the-bed-all-weekend," the guys retreat into TV sports, alcohol, and sleep. Just bad timing on everybody's part all the way around. Yeah, if I was lookin just for sex, life would be a lot simpler with my younger men. But I just want more this time to come in the package. Somebody with some energy and a sense of humor, who's read a book and loves me cause he can't help himself. You know, somebody with a little zip. I'd love him back. I swear I would."

Throwing back her long black, layered hair that drifted to her hardened shoulders, Siedah pushed her bare feet through the iron grate fence of the restaurant Intrigue's porch.

She came to the Quarter each summer to remind herself that she was black. She came during the summer because Mardi Gras in February was a drunken, insulting mid-western tourist festival that made the summer tourists look like saints. It was sometimes easy to forget that one was black in these early 21st-century days of asserting one's "humanness" over other things one was, thus nourishing the very dangerous notion of believing that one's world no longer made qualitative and deadly judgments based on one's color. Oh, the black dysfunctionals she'd seen let loose on the world after their sheltered college days were over!

She remembered reading about the black supervisor who'd had sex with ten or so of his white female team members and who, frankly, felt each and every one of them would die for him. When he chose to side with the black line workers in the car plant in their racism suit against management, the white women—his lovers—of course threatened with the loss of their jobs by white, male upper-management, came to tell Joe Negro that "certain information," especially the "constant harassment" he had subjected them to that had pressured them into "abnormal," "deviant," and "bestial" sexual practices, would be revealed to the white boys *and* the black line workers he had sided with. It wouldn't look too good for those other blacks who were trying to get into management, since, as everyone in business knows, one black human being represents the faults— never the merits— of every nigger from Johannesburg to Tacoma. And those line workers would quickly turn against him.

He would be seen by the blacks as just another Uncle who had abused his privileges as house Negro to ignore them and go to bed with Massa's property. The Boys wanted no less than he go to these obstinate nigra— whose case was air tight *on paper*— and convince them it was best for them and the company if this suit were dropped: the tidbit would be added that those who aided Joe would be the very two or three (out of 20,000) who would be promoted to supervisors, thus making any future suits moot. Oh! Joe saw the shrewdness that became inherent to those who for more or less two thousand years had grown adept at kicking darker human beings in the ass.

And the psychiatric-session-inducing-part of the whole mess was that was all so antithetical to what his parents had taught him ("Love everybody and they'll love you back"), what the church had taught him ("The Lord will always protect you from your oppressors"), and what he had believed in those glorious days of college: ("I am just like white people, just darker, an extra-superficial difference at best, and if I am in fact just like them and treat them with love and respect as I would any black person, then they will treat me with the same respect they would give to any white person— which I'm sure is general and good"). And oh how college had nurtured these ideas of equality, with its equal grading system, interracial sex protected by co-ed dorms and high walls, and its all-black basketball team with its all-white audience. Surely, college must have been only a microcosm of the rest of the real world. And he had gone off with his good grades and his natural charisma and found a great job immediately because of the melanin content of his skin, with that government pressure on his company and that government money pouring in for company grants, which, of course, all of his white supervisors took credit for and moved up the ladder based on their great sense of equality.

And then, there he was, caught between family and friends. The lawyer read to the local media the explanatory note he'd left. 24 hours after he'd been given his ultimatum, the note was all that was left of Joe.

So Siedah was determined never to let what seemed like acceptance and success deceive her into believing that she was not what the powers of her society would continue to regard her to be. Even harder and superficially contradictory, she was determined, at the same time, to become and remain exactly what her self-perception dictated and forecast she be: perfect, fresh, and never-before-known.

In other words, an African-American.

* * *

A job is a job when you've got no money coming in, so of course Zip went directly to Peninsula Airlines because he'd heard on the AM station that they were hiring reservationists. A job was a job, but reserving things for other people was a part of what Zip was running away from. A job was a job until the pressures of same started complimentarily giving you stress, fat, 6 packs a day, a fifth of 151 a day, sleepless nights and a limp peter. Then it was no longer a job. It was a death sentence that you labored at 24-hours-a-day to fulfill. So Zip saw his tenure as a reservationist as finitely as possible. 3 months at most, 3 weeks preferably, until something broke for him. And what was it that Zip was waiting to break?

Well, bless his soul, the boy could sing! He figured a couple of **DONNEL**-oriented auditions in Afro-centric Atlanta, and he'd have a job in a middle-echelon hotel, maybe $500 a week; a month of that, and word would mercury uptown that there was a Memphis man, well-built with natural tan, making women re-evaluate their marital commitments in hotel lounges in Buckhead, Decatur, etc. Then he'd be asked to play the big-time hotels at maybe $1000 a week, and then from there, who knew? Miami? Atlantic City? Vegas even? He lacked no singularity of purpose or intense belief in himself as Chosen. He was black, brave, and oh-so-bold. In his mind he was truly a new Negro for old. The hard part, as he already knew, would be convincing other people of his celestialness; people who thought the high points of a weekend were Saturday's lawn-mowing and Sunday's afternoon trip to Cream Queen.

Further, making a living doing something which wasn't too hard, didn't degrade him, and which gave him a chance to express his urban and human self while building toward making a lot of money, would also give him a chance to really make a decision on what would give his life some kind of emotional base of operation; y'know, a reason to live. And while he had no exact notion of what this would be, his brain was not so clouded by his search and the heat of his system that he could not see what his "reason to live" could *not* be made of:

1) U.S. blacks were still an irritant everywhere in the world; there was not now, nor had there ever been, nor would there ever be again, anything quite like them. Everyone, even Africans, wanted one. They were like the latest Parisian fashions— except even better cause Afro-Americans never seemed to go out of style. They were style. And for simply being the type of human he was he aroused the utmost hatred and fascination— at the same time— from people whose opinions mattered; that is, people with money. Zip would carry this fact with him always, whether he wanted to or not, like a cross— or a medal.

Thus, for him to assume that he should live for the day when he would be "accepted" by his society, a Caucaso-centric society which even discarded whites if they were not productive economic units, was absurd; like anxiously waiting for pay-day on the 32nd of each month.

2) Relatedly, life was finite; you were a mortal. You couldn't help it. You lived a few years, then you died. Yet your mind seemed immortal, with plans for a good life "later on" extending infinitely in front of your feeble efforts at a good life in the present. And you had to decide that you were not going to be paralyzed by racism and a strange economic set-up which gave the most to those who needed more the least. So basing his happiness on the belief that if he lived long enough, things would just naturally get better, left him empty;

3) almost as empty as traditional concepts of God left him. Blacks prayed to Jesus all day and all night every Sunday; and they had always prayed and they always would pray, and on Monday they would go back to their minimum-wage jobs and pray some more. But He never came down and undid all the stuff blacks prayed and sweated against on Sunday. But they kept on praying. And then they died. Zip was pretty sure that if there were a God, he was the head of the largest oil company in the world; he wore a spotted-red, clone tie, drove a Rolls, and he was out on the lake, resting, on the Seventh Day, no phone on the yacht. This explained why He never answered all that praying and shouting. So religion was out as a reason to live. In religion your reason to live was to die so you could go to heaven and live.

4) Believing in a career did not even warrant the mental electricity it took to materialize the ridiculous image. In these times, if one did stumble into some kind of corporate position, it was absolutely at the bottom of the money and status heap, and only a lunatic would believe that there was really a chance of "getting ahead;" the boss would tell you up front that the job was temporary in form as well as fact. If you attached your self-esteem (or any long-term bills) to a system, you may as well have attached it to a lead weight and smilingly submerged yourself in drudgery, never to come up for air— or investments— again. Belief in careers as sustaining factors of life defied the fact of 95% of all old people dying alone and in poverty. If it ever did, a job no longer saved your life. With its excessive labor and dehumanizing corporateness, a job went back to being what it always was before the rich invented the illusion that a job— any job— gave meaning and happiness to life: a job became immutable drudgery that no longer saved your life, but took it.

and 5) working in conjunction with all these facts were two more contradictions: a) LIFE, as Zip saw it, was a big joke, in which you pulled off a few little pranks of relative merit or embarrassment, never reaching the punch-line, and then you left your children to do the same things, and they left their children, and so on. Yet, he desperately wanted to be a part of this system of belief a few people at the top had constructed, with all its money-lust and class rituals and dead-end jobs. He saw through it all, But he had an attachment to LIFE as long as he could be allowed to share in its positive illusions; and b) If he got into LIFE and remained a part of the illusion, he was sure he could disrupt it by knowing its secrets. And that way he'd find a way out of the bad illusion that everyone just played along with, and construct a good illusion of his own. And his illusion would be real and true. The bad illusion, which he temporarily wanted to be a part of, denied any reason to live. But the good illusion was reason enough to want to stick around.

* * *

As he walked toward *THE FLY INN*, near the airport, Zip projected his self-image to himself; he shot the projection off the back of his skull, out of his eye-sockets, and onto the service entrance door. The combined physical and spiritual emanation that knocked on that door was typically African-American: one-third id founded causatially on nothing but intrinsic human-worth, one-third sweat and hope, and one-third Voodoo-video tape.

"Is the owner in?" he asked the walking-dream-waitress who came to the door.

"Yeah, well, whacha want withim?"

"Look, umma singer and I can back myself up on synthesizer. I saw your sign saying 'LOUNGE WITH LIVE ENTERTAINMENT', and I was just wonderin, mam, if the owner had time to give me a listen?"

"Well what kinna stuff you sing baby?"

"I sing mostly ballads, love stuff, Dee Dee Bridgewater, Rene & Angela, Marvin Gaye, **DONNEL**, Marsha Wright, y'know. But, I mean, I can rock too."

"Naw Naw honey. If you sing **DONNEL** I wanna hear it. God, honey I miss **DONNEL**! That was a shame the way **DONNEL** died last year. Got himself down to 165 pounds, and then that fat woman in Cincinnati jumped up on stage and sat on him. Crushed him as flat as a chocolate coin. I guess our haints always come back to get us. Anyway, Mr. Hugh's back in the back in Mr. Hugh's office. You come on in and sit at the piano and I'll get Mr. Hugh."

After getting through the lobby, Zip understood why they had a half-dozen passenger car-seats up front with little tables in front of them. Inside was a theme lounge named **THE SUPER FLY!** Oh it was great. The seating in the entertainment area was made up entirely of circa 1965-75 Cadillac car seats. Each one had a little arm rest in the middle and had been reupholstered with fake leopard and zebra skins. The tables were car dashes with legs attached, and the dance floor was roped off by seat-belts. In each corner there were video monitors that perpetually showed the movie *Super Fly*. And the bathrooms! There were little car mirrors to look into and the toilet tops were car air-filter covers. Little car ashtrays were scattered everywhere and car floor mats covered the floor.

Looking at the menu, Zip saw that their mixed drinks were also unique. One could order a "Brim" (giant tropical drink in a hat-shaped glass with drambuie and light Creme), a "Super Fly" (served hot with dark and light rum, in a boot-shaped glass with stacked glass heel) or a "Freddy's Dead." Its contents were not listed.

The hostess reappeared.

"Mr. Hugh wants you to come on back. Mr. Hugh's name is Mr. Hugh. P.S: Look Mr. Hugh in the eye when you're talkin to Mr. Hugh. Mr. Hugh don't trust nobody won't look Mr. Hugh in the eye."

"Thanks."

"Anything for somebody who can sing like **DONNEL**, baby. See you later." And she pointed to her left down an unlighted hallway. At the end of the hallway was a closed door covered in red-padded leather, so it was impossible to knock. The bass voice boomed "Come on in" just as the flat of Zip's palm slapped the leather. Behind the door was an enormous office 20' x 40'. The panelled walls were covered with pictures and broadsides of performers, some of whom could be seen hugging the proprietor.

The owner was 7 feet of black man named Mr. Hugh. Mr. Hugh was all Mr. Hugh was called. As far as Mr. Hugh's employees knew, Mr. Hugh had no 1st name. Furthermore, no one could possibly have known Mr. Hugh well enough to call Mr. Hugh by a 1st name other than "**MR.**" Mr. Hugh introduced Mr. Hugh as Mr. Hugh. Mr. Hugh spoke in the third-person of

Mr. Hugh as Mr. Hugh.

"Mr. Hugh is glad to meet you son. Girl tells Mr. Hugh you can sing. That so?"

Zip was still standing. He hadn't been asked to sit, and he wasn't going to sit until that gigantic man in the black suit told him to sit down. Musta been 15 yards of black silk on the man.

"Yes sir, I can sing. I've sung in clubs before." A big lie.

"Sing **DONNEL**?"

"Yes sir. I can sing "Ain't Done Yet," "Hard Time Coming," "Hardest Thing To Do," and "Touch and Go." I can sing all the ballads and I can spice it up if you want me to. Prince's love songs. Marsha Wright's sexy stuff. Whatever you want and how you want it sir."

"Sit down boy." Mr. Hugh pushed Mr. Hugh's big, red-leather office chair back against the wall. The springs over the wheels groaned as Mr. Hugh leaned back. Zip pulled a small office chair over to the desk and sat.

He was trying to look into Mr. Hugh's eyes. There was one small problem with that.

Mr. Hugh wore sunglasses that were absolutely opaque. Zip's expensive Ray Bans had automatically cleared up for the inside, but Mr. Hugh's glasses looked like the ones Muslims wore in Chicago in 1965. What to do? Look at the spot just below the glasses? He felt silly looking right into the lenses, and occasionally the glasses caught the reflection from the lamp on the right of Mr. Hugh's desk, and it was like trying to look into one of those mirrored disco balls. Zip stared at the lenses.

"The lounge is really only busy on Friday and Saturday nights. Those are the nights you'd work 9-11 and 12-2. Mr. Hugh's got a boy in there workin those slots now, but he's gotta go. Fool broke out with some crazy-ass song last weekend. 'Original composition' he called it. Damn song was called 'No Pussy Blues'. Mr. Hugh's got enough problems without Georgia Vicers comin in here pullin Mr. Hugh's liquor license for lewd goins on. Anyway, he through. Letim go back to what he used to do, English professor or somethin like that. Starvin when Mr. Hugh hired him. Anyway, you go on right after Peggy. She plays the piano from 8-9 every night.

"Mr. Hugh wants it right, tight and clean; don't show up late and don't show up high. Play to the customers, givem what they want. Start you out at $75 a night. If you work out, Mr. Hugh can do some other things. Right now, Mr. Hugh wants to hear some of the stuff you're gonna give the folks."

"Right now?"

"Ain't no time like now. Now is when everything is happnin. Let's you and Mr. Hugh do it to it. Mr. Hugh likes you boy. Mr. Hugh likes people who look Mr. Hugh in the eye. Got to look life straight in the eye even when you can't see it clearly. That way, when you get old, you got some honor, even if you been beat. You did your best, y'understand."

Mr. Hugh followed Zip out to the stage.

Love songs didn't come out right for Zip unless there was a woman around he could try to melt down.

"Excuse me mam, my name is Zip Peters and I appreciate the way you handled me when I came in… could you do me a favor Miss… what is your name?"

"Peggy."

"Oh, you're a performer too."

"Honey, umma hostess, waitress, cook and manager. But what I wanna do and what I do best in life is play the piano. Course, I do what I wanna do round here cause I'm Mr. Hugh's daughter."

Zip froze, staring into her eyes. And in the few seconds it took between the time he heard her desires and the time he could express his, "The Piano Lady" circuited through a synapse, and it was 1987 again.

* * *

Oakland, Tennessee is 30 miles northeast of Memphis, and it is a quiet, pretty, and completely unremarkable, rural place, except that that's where all of Zip's ancestors seemed to come from. Joneses and Burnetts and Peters, and there were hundreds ofem. Blacks, poor and rural, and living out existences which make for good black novels and good black movies if you're in the mood for 3 or 4 hours of screaming, crying, and gnashing your teeth.

However, just on the edge of Oakland, before Sommerville and after Eads, was a house painted bright pink. To all who observed her and created the legends about her, the person who lived in this house did not live a mule-like existence, as did every other colored person in the area.

This was the Piano Lady. No one really knew the history of the Piano Lady, and this is what made her an emblem of emulation. She appeared, as though from nowhere, with a clean 3 bedroom, wood house, with a real roof (not tin) and beautiful blooming roses in the front yard. Inside, all the furniture seemed to be first-hand and store-bought.

And in the front room was a piano.

Not some used, beaten-up and out-of-tune upright piano from some juke-joint in Eads, but a goddam shining, Steinway. It was wider than a cotton wagon. If she had flown up into the August night sky and broken off a boulder from the Moon and set it in her living room, the miracle to the black people around Oakland could have been no greater than this expensive big black thing sitting in the Piano Lady's front room. Other than the piano, its bench, and piles of sheet music under the bench, there was nothing else in the room.

Other positive rumors surrounded this pink home. The Piano Lady owned her own land. She didn't sharecrop. Money came from her playing, but could it have been enough to pay for all this? She had no husband and no children, and she wasn't a prostitute. There was a cold-drink machine on the porch that people could use 24 hours a day— a nickel for a Coke, Frosty Rootbeer or an orange or grape Nehi. And the woman, herself: 45-ish, with skin the color of copper and long black hair, doubled and redoubled into a bun at the back, and braided, going down the top of and inside her blouse and down her back; her figure big and robust, a country-girl, but still with all the right curves to go into her store-bought dresses; light-brown eyes and lipstick redder than the color of hot-peppers in September.

On Friday and Saturday nights, she played in her front room anything the people standing around the piano and standing in her front yard wanted to hear. From those hits and the songs she had written herself, they all learned of the city, and all the things the country was not. Most times the city was Memphis, but in any song on any night the city might be any city— Atlanta, New Orleans, Chicago, Detroit, D.C., even New York— anywhere that a colored person might get paid enough to actually live on. She herself was a city woman and no one knew from what city and no one cared. But she was everything they wanted to be and were not.

And who was that in the back seat of that '56 Buick Special every weekend for that entire special summer, only half awake some evenings, listening to the Piano Lady and humming along, memorizing words, watching the people sweat and sing along? Who was that up from Memphis every weekend that summer because his mother's cousin, Virginia, the last of her family un-urban, was ill and needed care? Who was that in that summer, only a few years after blacks finally became fully human on paper, 4 feet tall and 80 pounds of trouble, with a rope of braided hair not cut in 9 months because his mama promised God she wouldn't cut it for a year if

He kept her child alive past his fractured skull— jumping on the back seat out there those nights, after his father had insisted that he and his wife take a break after tending to the sick all day— even then learning how to push a note from the top of his throat to the bottom to play his listener's scale of emotions like a piano?

The Piano Lady had somehow found the key to satisfaction in *THIS* life, and that boy knew that she had. Later, music had been the only thing he could use to evoke her essence, now so long gone in fact, and music was the only thing he could use to keep in touch with his boyhood world that was so much better than the world he was currently stranded in. This boy sang to live, and because every note came from every micro-milliliter of his soul, he sounded like Nat King Cole with cream.

Who was that boy?

* * *

"— cause I'm Mr. Hugh's daughter... Zip, Zip! You ok? Honey, what's wrong?"

"The Piano Lady. Huh? Yea um ok um ok. I just... look, will you stay and listen while I play for Mr.— I mean, your daddy? I really would appreciate it."

"May as well. I was gonna clean off the bar anyway. You sure you ok?"

"Fine, fine. You just reminded me of somebody who was alive. That's all."

* * *

In New Orleans, summer was just about over, and Siedah was humming **DONNEL'S** last album of songs to herself as she slinked down Canal Street. She was on the prowl.

Chapter 4

A LONG DATA DVD FROM SIEDAH NEVER PLAYED

"<u>SUNDAY</u>:
For You:

It's difficult to describe what happened to me to turn me into the person I am now. I used to not need anything from anyone and then I hit 35 and BOOM: all of a sudden I needed to love and be loved in the dumbest cinematic sense of the phrase cause in a dream he came to me and the feeling was so good that I knew that for a girl like me who ain't never had enough of nothing that the new feelings in that dream were better than the old feelings outside the dream and I knew I wanted to keep the new. It's like when they first came out with that Play-n-View TV a few years back: after that, why would you want to watch the action anymore when you could be a part of the action just by stepping into it?

In college I read all my Camus of course, but itsa big difference between memorizing and comprehending. And all of a sudden, years later, I comprehended what Absurd was all about. What are we doing here with the little bitty time we have? What *do* we do here? Are we doing anything of any importance at all, even the ones who are rich and powerful? Or are we just here for a minute like moths, and we go and that's the end of us. Now, that's Absurd. All our memorizing geometric theorems, groaning, and plucking our eyebrows for nothing… nothing done to give any significance to the moths that follow us. Then, right then, I felt all my living—all my life—to be completely Absurd, without a trace of reason.

It's so goddamed pointless to live for money at my age. First of all, you can never get enough of the stuff, and when you're done compiling it, nobody sees your emptiness clearer than you do cause *you* know that nobody in this world ever made a pile of money honestly, and honesty was that thing you left on the shelf with your Easy Bake Oven.

So I figured there's gotta be something permanent that you can throw your temporary self into, and one morning I woke up and this time my eyes weren't still shut; I knew what the something was: *"Love is like a walk down Main Street,"* Al Green sang, and he made me want to lay on that lyric all day.

I realize now I have so much I want to say and so many ways I want to say things that I know I won't complete this recording tonight. I'm going to have to give me some time. Right now, um gonna take this sweating, naked body into a very cold shower, stick my head under the spray, and rethink my dream 3 or 4 hundred times. Then again, maybe I'll just stay in bed with this dream for a while, since I'm already naked and all.

MONDAY:

They say some things are better left unsaid, and, well, I guess that's right cause Lord knows I've said some things that I wish I could grab back and stuff down my throat. But since I don't know you yet, don't know if I ever will know you, I figure I can just say what's on my mind, and if you wanna later use my openness against me to close me, I'll just have to take that chance cause I gotta speak.

Love is a smile. And it's one of those smiles that comes when you don't expect it and you can't make it stop. In the emptiest and easiest part of my life, at a time when to be a success all I had to do was stay out of the rock house and not go to bed with white women's husbands, when cool breezes blew in from the Gulf in the heart and heat of July and my condo doubled in its FHA estimate, during the point where my most stressful days occurred when I had to choose between the taupe or the black high heels and every design and blue-print I put together was a hit and my co-workers weren't jealous enough to even *say* anything bad about me, when the ugliest part on my body was my 24K diamond ring, and when the Saints had finally gotten into and won the Superbowl, in a dream you came to me and I could not resist you.

Did my need and longing conjure you up? Did I make you come just to make me come? Or were you already entityied out there and came to me cause you felt me and flew straight into my flame? Baby, you know my aloof attitude is just a chain-link fence I hide behind, and while you can't break it down, you don't have to. You can just get me through the cracks.

So if you wanna hurt me, you know it's not very hard to do, but what I really, really want from you is to see me through and stop lettin me be this halfa person. You know you'll haveta fight me all the way, but baby your victory is really ours, and I'll pay you back by knockin down your walls too.

TUESDAY:

One time when I was 12 I went walking to the store. I had on my blue sailor's dress with the big, white, floppy collar and the naval insignia on it. Behind my back was a big, blue, cotton bow that was tied around my waist and bounced around on my already-round behind. I was already a 32-D and my legs were better than my mama's. I had only two strong desires in life: to go to DisneyWorld and spend the night in Michael Jackson's suite, eating up all his jelly beans and coffee ice-cream, and the other desire my parents didn't even allow me to think about.

So I'm walking down St. Charles and whistling some old **DONNEL** and I see some BOYS. BOYS I wasn't supposed to talk to; BOYS I wasn't to receive phone calls from; BOYS and BOOKS didn't mix; BOYS only wanted one thing and it was a bad thing and I wasn't supposed to want it either; BOYS started with the same letter as Bad-news, Backasswards, and Bad Breath; and I was supposed to only think of C words like church, chaste, cute, children, college, careers, and … chain-link fences.

These BOYS always teased me cause I never said a word to them and I was so cute and cuddly. None of us woulda known what to do with ourselves if I had given them some, but I sure woulda been tryin to figure out what to do. Plus, it was so easy just to flip my nose up at BOYS cause they always gave themselves away. Men are so transparent. If they want you, they tell you so, and then they're at a complete disadvantage. And since all of 'em are alike, I was perpetually the girl in a toy store with all the money and time in the world. But you have to play with a toy before you can know if you like it or not, and daddy had told me I better not ever get ready to play with these toy-boys or he'd put me on punishment.

So they started out as usual, saying stuff like "Uh uh uh, why don't you let me buy you something at the store pretty girl," and "Hey baby can I walk with you?" and "Hey Siedah, just tell me what it would take!"

"More than you have," I'd think to myself on the first-level response, but always thinking something opposite on a deeper level. But I'd never say a word.

And I just kept walkin and threw my little button up in the air. But I musta really looked like myself that day cause this day when I threw my head back I saw all of 'em come runnin toward me, and before I knew it they were in a circle around me—not really threatening me in any way—but just lettin their testosterone and my navy dress get the best of them, taunting me.

They said things like, "Why you won't never talk to us?" and "You ain't better than us little girl, you just a lot prettier," and "Why you never sit next to us in class or at lunch? You too fine to even eat with us?" and "Why you so stuck up?"

And then I started to cry and onea the BOYS said "Uh oh," and they all ran away in one direction and I ran away in the opposite direction.

But what I couldn't do, what I couldn't tell them is that I was crying cause I wanted to run in their direction, with them. But then everybody in the world woulda dumped on me, including them and including me. I felt so unstuck cause I just wasn't like what I was spozed to be like.

Shoot, I'd been having all this sexual energy since I was 9, and I just didn't have no place to put it. But I got a feeling mama musta been just like me when she was little cause I was just out playing in the yard one day when I was 13 and I saw her staring at me through the window, and all of a sudden she came out and snatched me and took me to her gynecologist and she attached to my lower left side onea them then-new time-released birth-control patches, and I didn't even know what it was until I was 15; I just thought I had sprung a leak somewhere or something. But the whole episode set me on some deep thinking about what mama was really like and what she had always pretended to be like cause she was only 13 years older than me.

And I would see BOYS walking in front of my yard or at school that I really, really liked, and I knew I wanted to make love to'em and I knew I'd be clumsy at it but that I'd make up for that in enthusiasm. And I knew that sex was for me.

But always over my shoulder was my society tellin me that good girls didn't even think that way, much less actually did it; and at the same time tellin me that black girls were all whores anyway, pressuring me to sit on my pussy to disprove a point that was a lie in the first place. Contrary to what you see on the street corners, we're the most puritanical people in the U.S. cause we're always trying to live up to or live-down stereotypes instead of being ourselves.

And if I looked to the left, there were mama and daddy tellin me that I couldn't even feel nothin like that til I was 21 and that when I did feel that way it had better be for one man with a good job forever-and-ever-Amen; and on my right were my girlfriends all still wanting to play jacks and watch the Disney Channel, and all the BOYS sticking out their obnoxious little pre-pube tongues and makin it too easy for me; and straight ahead in the mirror was me, looking all confused and gettin down on myself because by society's definitions I was an 18-year-old BOY trapped in a 13-year-old girl's body.

So when I finally found out what that patch was for at 15, I got as secretive as Amon, and nobody never knew that I had finally been allowed to find myself, and I was happier than I had ever been. I finally had some place to put what I was feeling, and child, I put it every place I could.

I confided in granny about the whole funny ordeal just before she died last year, and she burst out laughing and spit her snuff into a Maxwell House Coffee can and held me by my hand and said:

"Look, *I* don't understand all this new waiting around to do it anyway. Why do you think all of us from back in the country got married at 11 and 12? Honey child, my idea of fun ain't sittin on a active volcano. You got to let that lava flow to cool it down. Don't tell your crazy-ass mama though. That po child! She's only 11 years younger than I am and she done got so un-black that I think she wants to think the Smurfs brought her here in a mushroom."

* * *

And now look at me Night-Time Lover. All that good stuff that made me so happy for so long just ain't enough by itself no more. I want you.

WEDNESDAY:

I couldn't get you off my mind today. As I pulled the Porsche into the parking garage, I just left the radio on and lay back and thought of you.

Fantasies are almost always better than the real thing. And even when the real thing is there and lives up to your desires, it can be pretty scary sometimes. Hard to pull back from the real thing, hard to control it. But in my fantasy in my car, you loved me the way I wanted to be loved.

It's a pretty simple equation, but it's so hard for most people to work out. Here it is—uh—

Step 1: you loved me as much as you loved yourself—uh—

Step— uh—2: you wanted me to do well in life, and none of your own insecurities   would make you want to undo me—uh—

Step 3: you always remembered what we were in the game for in the first place: TO GIVE EACH OTHER FUN, not to turn each other into our own parents and grow old and die.

—uh—Step 4: you were always around when I needed you

and

Step 5: you always gave it to me like we wouldn't be gettin a chance to do it again— uhhh!

THURSDAY:

My immediate game plan right now is simple: find you, fuck you, and feel for you forever. I can really appreciate those kinna life-enhancing feelings on a day like today that was filled with those feelings' opposites.

I know lots of four-letter words, but the dirtiest and most dehumanizing one I know is W-O-R-K. W is for **wasting** my human-potential slaving for superiors who don't do a quarter of my work-load and whom I never see; O is for **only** making more money for people who need more money like I need more tits; R is for **running** like a rabbit on a treadmill that never ends if you have one honest microbe in your psyche; and K is for **co-workers** who hate me cause um blacker, cuter, smarter, and make more money cause I work harder.

Anyway, I know you don't want to hear all this, but um afraid that's gonna be a part of loving me too. You know how it is. Sometimes you just need somebody to tell it to.

FRIDAY:

I can't decide if this would be the best night to be with you or if it would be Saturday night. I think maybe Friday cause we could dance off the work week and later retire and do some… reading. I wrote a poem for you at work today and here it is. I hope you like it:

THREE IMAGES FROM AN IMAGINED SELF-PHOTOGRAPH
1. PLACE

Tonight I have on a pair of black panties
and a red sweat shirt the color of the flesh
of a Texas Grapefruit,
and I think to myself,
"Aren't those the colors of the flag of Egypt?"

I think not.

But how appropriate that I think of Egypt,

because tonight I am thinking of you,
and those trips to Mëroé,
and the photographs you take there,
and the people and the ruins,
and a look on your face from a self-photograph that says,
"This is where I want to be with you."

I am thinking of you tonight.

And I think, again, it is not so much the place,
as it is the feeling of mind
that keeps you contented, so dissatisfied.
Your face says, "I feel comfortable here."
Your face says, "I look cool
running my fingers on these glyphs."
Your face says, "I like an expedition filled with dreamers."
Your face says, "I want you."

I am thinking of you tonight.
Your thoughts grab me around the waist
where the two colors of my Egyptian flag panties and shirt meet,
and my face says, "Yes."

2. TIME AND DREAMS

Before we know each other's last names,
before we have a drink,
before we ever say more than ten words at one meeting,
before we ever write letters,
before we ever sleep together,
and I know the luscious mole on your back,
and every beige crevice that leads from your curved bottom,
so like a warm and soft blue Matisse,
up your back to your hard shoulders
that end in a high, wide turn just below your brown eyes,
so full of light,
and more natural than the quiet forest they imitate,
where your mouth blooms full in the spring,

I dream you.

And we talk all night in a polished nightclub
of white and silver.
And I in my purple satin bodice
trying desperately to remember lines of poetry,
and you in a sleeveless blue and black shirt
talking quietly, quietly, about history and dreams.

3. SELF-PHOTOGRAPH: DESCRIPTION AND NARRATION

Your self-photographed image now rests on my dresser.
In a silver frame, you lean against a wall of white and gray,
that is more the blinding remainder of your comet's wake,
than it is a solid thing.

In my present,
a striped pillow braces you against the wall of light,
And your braided, black hair, pushed to your right side
to hang on your hardened shoulders,
does not fly back in your cosmic rush.

Seeing beyond the glass, your eyes envelop my bedroom,
always keeping me in the center of their vision.
And your bare shoulder points a photographer's eye
to your tank-top of combed white cotton,
which does not move, which does not fold,
as a calf as smooth and as hard as mahogany
glides beneath the silver frame.

In my future, this impish face of an Ishmael Reed hero
shall push its way through my bedroom walls.
It cannot be restrained here.
But I shall hold onto that wall of crackling light,
and then I shall be, always, always, within its silver boundaries.

SATURDAY:
Y'know, I was on this project recently. Somebody wanted to keep the

basic structure of this old club that had been closed down and build a pizza joint on top of all of it. Since the club was on the 2nd floor of this building, I went over there in Storeyville to see if the basic structure were strong enough to support counters, ovens, refrigerators, juke boxes, things like that. And it was strong enough, but I really hated to do the work on the project. I got choked-up in that old place.

The veneer on the floorboards of the dance floor were all scuffed and worn down. Those urban dance-floor guerrillas had left just one big rough groove in the middle of the club. And I thought, "We're gonna undo every trace of that groove, every trace of all that joy." And I just got choked-up and started to dance even though there was no music.

I never had an "urban revitalization" project affect anything on me except the size of my Money Market account. I don't know. It's hard to explain.

SUNDAY:
Missing you, and my recording time has run out.
Show up… or get out of my head."

Chapter 5

Inside of each of us is a kind of flicker or flame or desire— call it whatever you want to— that gives us the notion that we should do right things.

Somewhere along the way, between the time we think that life is endless and filled with red-balloons and music videos, and the time we die, alone, in an impersonal, blank room, with only the covered faces of emotionally-disattached strangers for company, we have to admit the impracticality of doing right and honorable things. Every black maid and butler who had ever lived since the fall of Memphis had been honorable and right and religious. And when they died—screaming—their children did not have enough money to bury them.

The grandchildren of these maids and butlers sometimes figured out ways to turn their labors into profit, but it was almost always at the destructive expense of less profit-inclined and less worldly blacks. Yes, the grandchildren of the maids and butlers were certainly in the black.

The most usual and numerous of such ostensibly honorable scams were the insurer, the medical doctors, or, the most disgusting of all, the politician. They were all smart enough to realize what they were doing to other blacks, but to make it economically in the society, at any price, was much better than not to make it. And everyone of every color knew that.

Sometimes some honest hustle would slip through the money-web and present itself, miraculously, to some down-trodden black, and he/she would be able to buy a home and a duplex and a Merc without destroying other blacks. Y'know, something like singing or honest preaching or playing some kind of ball, or pushing hair-care products, all areas where you did not have to depend on whites for your sustenance. But most times the avenues presented to blacks through which they could make more than minimum wage were all headed by whites at the top of that... pyramid, and to get within viewing range of the apex, you did the most unscrupulous things to other blacks because you would do *anything* not to go back to minimum-wage, rent, and total and complete powerlessness; and, as always, you could do these things to unmoneyed blacks because, as they had been since before recorded history, blacks were the most naive and trusting people this, or any other world, had ever known. Naivete coupled with trust: the deadliest combination in the world if anyone wanted to administer the poison.

One of the startling facts about the impracticality of doing right things is that it is much harder for whites to do right things than it is for blacks. One would think it would be easier for whites, as almost everything else is, because there are more economic opportunities for whites, and nobody sane would have a reason to do evil when the money is rolling in. But it's a bit more complicated than that. Job opportunities provide sustenance, but exploitation provides wealth. And even for the dumbest person in the world, there are always the trusting, religious blacks to exploit; and once this inescapable fact is discovered by bad people, the temptation for them to do wrong is often just too loaded with hard cash, prestige, and tax shelters to resist.

As is true for blacks who want to bother to try, there are remarkable white characters who find interstices in which to do right, and then there are whites whose characters are so magnanimously good that they refuse to do wrong even when blacks are on their hands and knees begging to be exploited.

These whites are not like the whites who give blacks minute loans at absurdly high interest, cause the blacks have no money and will take it at any cost; not like the whites who take black daughters who made the Dean's list in business management, and, because the job market is so depressed and because the girls don't know anybody, put the girls to work at various phone companies and reservations centers and fast-food outlets for minimum wage (now "finally" rolled back to $1.00 an hour); not like the black parents who beg illiterate white coaches to take their massive, black sons out to obscene places in the Bush of America where the nearest black cultural artifact is hundreds, and sometimes thousands, of miles away, so the sons can "naturally" and gladly sacrifice their knees for the Roman glory of those in the luxury sky-boxes. To the parents, all this was better than unwanted pregnancies, drugs, and joblessness. Of course, the whites who not only forego such opportunities for such exploitation, but who actively try to undo such exploitation, are about as numerous as Do Do's, and none are in any positions of power. Very few even have jobs.

Even more astounding is the anomaly of the poor white person who chooses to do right, when wrong is so effortlessly graspable. Poor whites had absolutely nothing material to gain, and every probability of gaining only poverty, by doing right in any context relating to blacks. Yet this odd, beautiful, self-destructive tendency continued to occur in some poor whites.

Such a celestial knucklehead was Dr. Dennis Johnston.

* * *

Besides Miss Scarlet and Jimmy Carter, Dennis Johnston was the strangest white person Georgia had ever produced. His family was so simple, dirt poor, and honest, that black sharecroppers and peach-picking migrants would take the Johnston kids in, wash them, feed them, and love them. Since there were 17 little Johnstons, this was no average act of magnanimity on the parts of people who averaged $600 a year in pay and had their own little pecks of children to feed and subdue.

But there was just something... something human about the Johnstons that made you love them. Why, right there in the middle of the United States' second Dark Age, known colloquially as the 1950's, these people seemed not to understand that they were white and that the people they befriended, even looked up to, were black.

On the fruit and cotton buses during picking season, from Tallahassee to Savannah, Thomas Johnston rode the same bus as the blacks, worked at the same shit-ass labor, and slept with men whom he knew to be his friends. He shared what little he had with them, as they shared with him, and he didn't look at their wives and they didn't look at his. Though, as one could see, Thomas obviously knew about sexual intercourse. But whether Thomas knew that sex led to the increasing number of small Johnstons that Emy Johnston was asked to herd around— well, this was something that no one was ever sure of.

"I think she's just that kinda gal," Thomas was heard to remark once. "As soon as she gets one out, she's due again. I wish we could get in touch with her ma and check and see how many her ma had. Um sure there's a set number for the girls in that family, but Emy don't know what it is; her ma ran off with a traveling Trojans salesman after 9 kids and before she was outta kid-bearing age. Emy says her ma woulda run off with a blind rat to get out of Georgia and away from those kids. Anyway, I don't give a damn. Lotsa fun wakin up in the mornin. One's got his big toe in your nose, nothern's got her finger in your ear, another pissin on your feet, one ofem draped over the headboard, another one screamin about the Booger Man in his sleep. It's bettern a circus and it's free!"

And every one of the kids so respectful and cute. They didn't look anything like Thomas and Emy, which gave them more of a shot at life than Thomas or Emy ever had. They came out round and sharp-featured and hairy and sweet, with big green eyes and dark-blond lashes, and they said "Yasm" and "Nome" to the black women who kept them when Emy was in the fields herself.

Of course, this whole nice family was doomed to tragedy. What are you gonna do with white people in America in the '50s who are poor, illiterate, believe if you're clothed, fed, and sheltered, then you're ahead enough, and who think black Americans are just as good— maybe better— than they are? Why, you run them into the ground of course! There was a certain natural order to things in Georgia in 1956, and while it was a good year for Chevrolets and the mental giant who invented hula-hoops, it was a very bad year for the Johnstons.

Thomas, after picking peaches all day for 50 cents, fell out of the back of the old truck the white farm-owner was driving; he fell out along with the other 8 black men he was sleeping with and on; he fell out because the wire they'd put in the truck's broken hatch-latch snapped, and out they spilled onto the highway. Drunk as a spinning top, on the farmer drove, thinking only of spending $4.50 for a day's labor from 9 men, and reaping $45 for the product of that labor. After the fall, Thomas' back was only good for lying back on; it sure wasn't any good for reaching up or bending down. There were still 5 children in the shack, the youngest being born the day Thomas hit that hard black-top, and so Thomas made himself useful by watching the kids while Emy went out for work.

Emy, 50 years old herself now, 13 births gone by, realized that the fields and orchards were no longer places for her. But in town, white merchants wouldn't hire her cause they'd have to pay her the same shit wages for the same shit jobs the black women were doing— they couldn't pay her more cause that would make the niggers upset with their pennies, and they couldn't pay a white woman less, cause that set an even worse example in front of the niggers. Black merchants, what there were of them, couldn't hire Emy, cause, first, it simply had never been done and they were afraid white men would burn their stores to the ground, and secondly, the black workers would have killed her, believing her to be a spy. Surely, a white woman could work anywhere she pleased, they would reason, while they, the blacks, worked only where white men told them they could work.

To them all, Emy presented the same plea, "If you let me work forya, I'll do a good job and I don't care what you pay me as long as you pay me.

I got to feed my family." But even with that plea to the worst and strongest instincts of any exploiter, she worked only sporadically and was paid even more sporadically.

The other 8 kids, all grown enough to leave home, did just that. They couldn't fit in with whites and they weren't allowed to fit in with blacks; uneducated, with agri-labor demand in swift decline, the boys reasoned that there was more sanity and honor in keeping Indo-China's domino from falling, and so they enlisted, little knowing that there are different degrees to hell, and the hell they were leaving behind was infinitely better than the one in which they would find themselves in a few years in some place called Vietnam. The girls heard about the department stores opening up in Macon and Atlanta and thumbed their way in those directions. You didn't have to have no education to work in a department store, they reasoned, just be white and know how to keep people from stealing stuff.

Of the 5 kids left at home on the day Thomas spilled out onto the black-top, the ages ranged from 11 to 1 day, and the 1-day-old had about as much chance at a substantial material and emotional existence as had any of the other kids, that is to say, not much, but still a chance. He was, after all, white, and all that had come to imply by that time in the United States. But the stupe was only white, poor and illiterate by circumstance, not, it seemed, by temperament or divine ordination. After Mama Mama taught him how to read the Bible in the back of her shack one day, the 5-year-old boy seemed on a mission: to undo by will what had been done to him by fate.

What a bold ass he was 2 years later as he stood at his dying father's bedside and told him that he was going to go away and find a school to go to— as soon as Thomas was through dying. What a fool he was to think that he could fit in with the citified-hick school boys of the public schools of Atlanta. What a miracle it was that he pulled his educational feats off under the pressure of staying with a sister who had only a lack of interest in his notion of getting an education.

And on and on this textbook Horatio Alger fantasy went. Always being the smartest, the brightest, working the hardest in school while working the hardest at the local open-air market to pay for clothes and supplies and such. Always working and reading and working some more, until there lay that academic scholarship on the table in 1974. Emory was a "good" school; that he already knew. What he didn't know was what he wanted to be the best in at the college. And after all the luck and the smarts and hard work, it just all played out at once, left him in the middle of the night it seemed, and when he woke up, the damn fool had decided to major in English and minor in music. This, my friends, is only one example of how the clone-tied God laughs at us through His Pouilly Fuisse.

Dennis compounded his idiocy exponentially, until now this graying, Western intellectual, much closer in genius and demeanor to Ellington than Eliot, found himself possessed of a Master's degree in music and a Master's and Ph.D. degrees in English composition, and completely and totally, now in the middle of the year 2017, as unemployable as a primordial ape who had just learned to discern night from day.

But he had a secret and energy—all in this world you need except love and luck—and those were all he needed as he dragged these nights from one rotten lounge and blues club to the next, thinking, thinking about what he knew.

* * *

If you could have felt as the Neanderthal felt when he found that knocking two particular types of stones together could make a shimmering, orange thing that would effectively fight off that other thing which turned his calves and loins blue, if you could have had Khafre's power to permanently reproduce his likeness before there *was* photography, if you could have been Buddha when he found that he never had to worry about having enough pocket change to see the universe cause he was the universe, if you could have been Lancelot on a Friday night, with Guinevere's light on in the tower window and Arthur out in the swamps looking for the Grail, if you could have been a French teacher in England in 1066, if you could have owned all the beachfront property at Plymouth and Jamestown around 1620, if you could have invented penicillin in 1750, if you had been shrewd enough to buy up all the patent rights to those strange looking things called "machines" in 1810, if your name could have been John D., Sr., before income tax and antitrust suits, if you threw a baseball for a living and your first name were Joe and your wife's first name were Marilyn, and if you had only been sexually-farsighted enough in 1979 to buy a condom company, then you would have been able to feel about half the joy and excitement that Zip felt as he stepped onto the performance stage on this evening that the Donhead had come to the **JUK** club for a special on-location shooting of <u>Black Train</u>. A child of the night from the beginning and still the carrier of enough monthly bills for a platoon, no sooner had Zip secured a gig at *THE FLY INN* than he had to moonlight.

Even in the bowels of his Soul Temple home that the DonHead had bought for himself in Inglewood (with a secret passage running 200 yards underground to emerge in the L.A. Forum with 4 reserved seats right behind the Laker Bench), the electricity of **JUK** had been felt. But even more, news of The New Kid In Town had whispered its way into Don's reverb-chamber, and both the boy and the scene had to be captured on the tape and the prefabricated set of the only black show on television that could perpetually stay on the air just by being itself. Black Train had become so big and the Donhead so bored in the 21st-century that he now often moved the whole set and group of dancers around the country to film with the latest talents-who-would-be-stars.

Zip pulled open the purple, metal door leading to the stage and saw that it had been painted with the big orange letters "DONHEAD PRODUCTIONS." He reached the edge of the stage and stood staring at the gathered Host. He had come just before the dancing was to be taped, and all the dancers stood or sat in a semi-circle with their backs to him. They were all listening to the DonHead. Everywhere, everywhere, was the golden glint of Negroes about to move.

An overwhelming bass voice seemed to fill the room and come from every direction. Its tempo was nerve-rendingly slow. This was the DonHead's method of making sure that everyone listened to him. His rumbling was like a giant, old clock, striking midnight: its slow drone could not be ignored; unless, of course, one were asleep, as were several of the nymphs and satyrs as the DonHead continued his discourse.

"Tonight's... taping... has... GOT... to... be... one... of... the... BEST... you've ever... done." Zip knew it would be a while before the dancers could get down to business. The oracular DonHead always took a while.

Zip sneaked around behind one of the big spots, but before he could get into a position to see the DonHead he was paralyzed. In front of him, facing the DonHead, with hands on hips were

... THEM. Yes. THEM. YOU know *exactly* who I mean. Even The-Tall-One-with-the-Pants-and-the-Caramel-Skin. She sported him a full rectal view as she turned around, leaned on a railing, and stretched her hamstrings and latissimus dorsi.

"Oh God, um not gonna make it to my set," he whispered. "Take me now Lord. Let my eyes die with this sight on their corneas, uh, uh, uh, uh, uhhh."

Zip held the base of one of the spotlights for support. He was dizzy. His years of monitor encounters with THEM had not prepared him for the flesh. His flesh was weak. He began to topple, knocking over the blue spot.

"What's this?" he heard the DonHead snarl. "Boy who you?"

"Ah, my name is Zip and I'm the singer who's supposed to come on after the opening dance sequences. Er, I just wanted to… watch."

Zip's voice had completely left him. His whisper was barely audible above the patrons' laughing and clanging glasses as they waited for something to happen in the club where something always happened.

"Ah-h-h, so that's what you look like. Yeah, you'll do for tape. Heard about you boy, that's why were're here."

Zip started to speak again, but The DonHead didn't talk to anyone more than 10 seconds.

"DANCE!" the DonHead shouted, and then the orange lights blended with the brighter purple and red ones, and the girls took their places on the formica locomotive and began to lay waste to the equilibriums of the men in the club the same way the taped version of their images would make all the husbands in America stay up after the Saturday night news to watch them so that these same husbands could get ready for bed with their wives.

Zip crawled onto the tall, black smoke stack of the locomotive and tried to get close to The-Tall-One-with-the-Pants-and-the-Caramel-Skin, but he could barely move. He was the kid turned loose in the toy store and all the toys had come alive and were playing with *him*. The gigantic speakers screamed out Michael Henderson's "Prove It," and Zip's soul exploded. Everyone was there: The Tall One, of course, The Hair, Total Bottom, Pretty Face, Pop Dress, Shoes-Slacks-and-Legs, Solid Stuff, Lower Locomotion, Purple Tops, Little Sister, and Costumes. Just one look was all it took, and he knew that the <u>Black Train</u> dancers had put enough fire in him for him to burn every woman in the place during his set.

* * *

Almost 6 feet and 180 pounds of nothing but body and energy, with his face as smooth as the spit-shine on his Stacy Adams, Zip oozed over the microphone.

"Um only what my lover wants me to be/
You know you can remake me/…"

"Debby will you look at that man. Where do they makem? I gotta get me a gross ofem. Mercy!"

"I don't know child, but he can sing to me in the bed, on the headboard, up under the bed, up under the house— "

"— Shhh! Will yall please shut up and let me hear the man? UH UH UH, just look at that chest will you?"

Zip's set had been extended from 20 minutes to one long hour at his request. His energy was so high and the vibes so right tonight that he knew, if given the time, he could make time stand still in that club. He could stop the clock. As he threw down, DonHead stood in the back in the corner in the dark and nodded. He knew exactly where this boy was going.

"I'll… have… to… get… another… ticket… in… the… Staples Center," Don thought to himself in his typical periodic fashion.

"And if we can just Relax awhile/
I know I can make you smile./

DO YOU WANT ME LIKE I WANT Y-O-O-OU?"

And back at Mr. Hugh's the next weekend, jealousy and possessiveness already rearing their Hydra heads in a leather-paneled 20' x 40' office, two days of singing extended to 7 at $1000 a week was alright for now.

* * *

Prof. Johnston's inculcated and innate knowledge had pushed him to discovering the source of the secret in the first place. And now that same knowledge turned into wisdom, as he dragged his shredding Adidas and fraying, scholarly, tweed-clad body through the Atlanta night air, being continually disappointed at the identities of the awful singers he found, but still searching with the memory of Mama Mama and his parents and so many good people like them moaning in the dark, nether-regions of his brain, reinforcing what he had already decided: that no one could use as much as he would get if he found IT, and that it was only right to try to share IT with the one who— by blood— should have IT in the present, and whose ancestors— ancestral ghosts now— suffered for IT and without IT in the past. Plus, you can't turn a lock without the key. He'd been to Memphis and he knew.

His key was singing somewhere in Atlanta.

Chapter 6

" 'D o this do that'— and all the time in broken English. Jim must think he my daddy or something and he ain't even close. He must be a goddamed fool. I do all my paper work the weekend before the week it's due and he doesn't even know— which is just the way I want it I guess. This NEGCO shit is getting old, old, old."

Resting her elbows on her Louis Vuitton purse, Siedah looked down from her seventh floor office window in N.O. onto John McDonaugh Park where she often jogged. City Hall bordered the park on the left; Gravier Street formed its limit on the right. Siedah saw the usual lunch-day routine. Black men cut the grass, cleaned up the grass, bagged it and carried it away. Black winos and street-men wandered in around the noon hour to ogle the thick-legged women coming out of City Hall for lunch. Occasionally, some kid tried to get a kite up between the intermittent rain showers. Siedah sighed.

Now, a lotta people search their whole lives for some kinda archetype they think they need to love, cause they need love to survive; it's just the nature of the romantic to have some ideal in mind and to whine and call into all-night radio talk shows to whine nationally until they could marry this ideal and then call in and whine some more cause the ideal they married could never, ever live up to the ideal they had conjured up before they were old enough to know what the verb "marry" meant. And, well, all of that was all right for *other* people, Siedah thought, but in her search for a man who would be worthy of her love she had put off all other sexual activity for two years, and no one was even coming close. Now suddenly a membrane parted that had kept hidden a drive that had always taken center stage before, and the breach in the dike could not be plugged.

With her horniness spilling out of her ears, she realized that her emotions had played her a dirty trick, at least as far as the way post-contemporary sexual liaisons are commonly done. Her emotions had connected sex to love, and now she wanted to love the guy she wanted to screw and nothing else close to that would do. Clearly, this was a handicap for which she hadn't bargained. It made work difficult and sleep impossible, and most irritating of all, the shit just wasn't logical. She'd never had this problem before.

And now she understood all those old Greek poems where the narrators begged the gods to keep them away from love— any atrocity could be borne except love— but even more important and more depressing to her, she finally could *feel* all those old blues songs about the problems of love, and that's enough to drive anybody crazy. Hearing the words and moving to the thump and watching the old, black singers groaning their hearts out for enough change to get back to their one-room, low-income apartments was one thing, but actually *feeling* what the singer sang, as the singer felt it and suffered for it, well, that was inhuman. Only a blues singer could live through it, and everybody knew there was never enough money to bury them.

"Maybe if I could just get a change, get away from New Orleans for a while. Get an assignment somewhere else. It'd give me a new attitude and a fresh crop of men to look over. Uh, how'd I ever get in this condition? Let me go check with Jim."

* * *

"DC-9's are a pain in the ass to fly. Narrow-ass aisles and no leg room."

Siedah stretched her ebon legs toward the cockpit, pushing her arms up and against the back of her seat. There were only a few people on the flight and it was late, and being business travelers, most of them were asleep. They'd all taken that hour's flight to Memphis before. Nothing new or exciting on the flight— except Siedah.

"Now exactly what is it I'm supposed to be researching up here?"

The way the boss had explained it to her, there were some old blueprints of an antebellum house in Memphis, a house burned down by someone for some reason toward the end of the Civil War, years after the city had been captured by Federal troops. On these prints were indicated the stress points of the roof of this very difficultly and elegantly designed mansion. This design happened to be the exact one that a NEGCO customer wanted his restaurant to follow.

"Southerners," Siedah mouthed audibly, remembering that she, too, was a native daughter, but a black sheep of the family, "how they flee to the past!"

Her father had told her about these oddly-shaped people who had congenital perception problems and the inability to find any chronological period in which they could feel comfortable. The future is only sketchily perceived as something worse than the present, and the present is not perceived at all, so Southerners stumble through it. Only the past was safe and rosy. They invented and lived in a romanticized DisneyWorld where everybody had good manners and was descended from some royalty somewhere, obviously, cause everyone was so refined. The ugly stuff was simply a misprint, a power surge that messed up the hard drive. Why, one could read entire "history" books about the Civil War written by Southerners that could cross-reference the actual number of buttons on Stonewall Jackson's coat on the day his own men blew a hole in him, and the same book could give you eye-witness accounts of the color of Bedford Forrest's kerchief as he conducted his massacre of civilians at Ft. Pillow, Tennessee. But the word **SLAVERY** would never be mentioned. And now somebody wanted to build a restaurant like some refined major's harem.

"Well, money's money baby, and that's what I work for. If this guy wants to build this monstrosity for people to eat in, I don't give a damn. We'd all be better off if we could all learn to be more like that. Throw decency and history and love-of-others-as-shown-in -love-of-self out the window to cater to peoples' basest desires and worship at the altar of cash money."

"This engineering is very odd. I can see it's supposed to be post-Sun King, middle 18th-century stuff, but something's not quite French about this thing. Let me check that architect's name and background again."

She was looking at a daguerreotype of the house in its prime, and at a drawing from the daguerreotype made by the restauranteur, he having aggrandized and speculated a bit on the floor plan of the house to anticipate its rebirth as a haven for fine French food in the epoch of the EAT-A-BURGER.

Siedah pulled papers from her briefcase.

"Yeah, well, you can't have a more French sounding name than that. Let me check this architect's bio again. Yep, yep, he's as French as Haiti. Born, bred, and schooled. But the slight curves in the descending plane of the roof, and the rounded ends of the gables as they cascade down, especially that weird right angle at the front. This design just doesn't fit for the 19th-century; looks more like it's from Nigeria—or a Saturn colony... unless. Wait a minute."

She turned the blurry daguerreotype more to a right angle and held it farther from her eyes. Perfect in everything else, Siedah was far-sighted. Examining the photo for several minutes, and then thinking and remembering her history of architecture classes, her mouth suddenly fell open.

"Well I'll be goddamed! I should have known! Leave it to blacks to figure some way to leave their signature on work that they knew their white owners would take credit for anyway. Some black men and women of West African, probably of Cameroonian descent, built this damn castle, but they purposely messed up the design— that is to say that they made it better by not following the dull blue-print. They made the roof resemble their own houses' curved cone tops by drastically arching the beams and sweeping under the gables. I mighta known. There's nothing to be done about us. The most obstinate people on earth. We leave jazz wherever we go, regardless of the conditions in which we must survive. The roof of the house is very similar to that one on the old Melrose Plantation in Natchitoches, Louisiana, and everybody admits blacks built that. I shoulda known. Now I'm interested in this job.

"Lessee, it was finished in 1860 before the war, and then some damn fool burned it down in 1864. But what the hell for? The rebels couldn't retake Memphis. Hell, the rebels couldn't retake a daguerreotype. If it were a Confederate, how did he get through the Union lines? Memphis had been a Federal post since it was captured in 1862, and the war didn't end until April of 1865 … whew, this is too heavy for my sleepy ass. I'll look this stuff over in the morning when I get to that research room at the public library. Let's see here, what was the name of it again? Oh yeah, the Memphis Room. How original."

* * *

He came to her at a glass-top table by the river, she in her neck-high, azure-blue silk dress, and matching heels too high to tell. She had been staring at the rapid pushing of the current and thinking of her desires and her dreams. With her high-tech mansion in the background, cement and steel, how serene this bluff seemed at night, as tall and as silent as the Peachtree Tower on Christmas Eve night, and as broad and as black as the Delta's expansive estuary as it emptied into the gulf.

And the Cruz '56 was so sweet as it touched her lips and tongue, and the breeze so warm as it floated her layered hair above those emerald ear-rings he came to her he did and sat at the opposite end of the table and stared into her black eyes oh it was days and then she said:

"Tell me why is it that you love me?"

And then she whispered "Now."

And he said, "I can't tell you why but I can tell you what for. I can tell you that sometimes love is an absence of complications and sometimes love is respect for personality and sometimes love is attraction to the soul and sometimes it's the you you see in the other and sometimes it's the coming from the same place and sometimes it's the kindness you've been shown and sometimes it's for the reasons I cannot or will not know and I can say I love you for all of that our body connection will be my launching pad and your sex will be our planet."

And she closed her eyes and whispered "Now" and he didn't have to ask because her love needed no expression because it had always been sure. And he came and stood beside her and touched her cheek and the night was never so black as it was at that moment and the waves sometimes licked at the old slave-hewn stones along the bank and the waves sometimes slammed against the laid stones and broke only the reflected light from the shore.

And he whispered "Now."

* * *

"Whew, what was that all about?" she whispered to herself.

Her dream had left her shaking, nervous all morning, wet as she drove from Front Street to Adams to Poplar, and still wet as she issued the requested ID's to the attendant at the Memphis Room.

That same dream she'd had recurrently for the past three years was starting up again.

* * *

"Ooo Zip! Everybody loves you. The women love you, Mr. Hugh loves you, and most definitely I love you," Peggy gushed, plopping down onto Zip's sweating, satined lap in the dressing room. "You're great, and um great with you."

"Baby, I got to admit you're right. WE ARE GREAT! I've got the greatest face, body, and voice in the world, and you're the best technological development to happen to instrumentation since the micro-chip… God, the past three years have been great. Mr. Hugh even pays me almost-human wages. I think I chipped a little paint off those glasses when I sang at ATLANTA NIGHTS, UP-TOWN ATLANTA, and the Ramada and Westin Plaza those coupla times. People throwin money and phone numbers at me. Pissed Mr. Hugh off good. Stood all the way up like a giraffe: 'Mr. Hugh thinks you done got pretty good boy— damn good. But don't you never think you bigger than Mr. Hugh. Mr. Hugh made you and Mr. Hugh can unmake you.' And then I said 'How much?' And Mr. Hugh said 'Whatever seems reasonable to you ... son. What you got in your throat can't be taught.' It's been wild—life personified— life as a human being. And I... think we might just be ready... but wait. WAIT-ONE-GODDAMED MINIT! Where's the white boy?"

"Zip what in the world are you talking about?"

"The white boy, we gotta get us one; we got to have one to say we're good. I don't care if we sound like a splice of Caruso and Aretha singin in heaven on a clear day with angels playing stereo-phonic harps, we ain't going nowhere until we get a white boy to say we sound good. Then we're good. Ask Smokey Robinson. He'll back me up."

"Well— you been puttin it off til you thought we were ready— do you want me to call daddy's friend at Asylum records in L.A.?"

"Is he white?"

"Ah... no."

Peggy pouted, and thought about the high notes they'd hit together, but never quite making the sounds for each other.

"Then he won't do. It kills me, but it's like that and that's the way it is... I don't know, I feel lucky tonight. A white angel might just drop into the club from the sky for the second set."

Chapter 7

"*Major Millbranch Winchester appeared from nowhere and invented himself in 1859. The white SOCIETY of Memphis, only recently having dredged themselves up from the sink-holes of eastern Arkansas, west Tennessee, and north Mississippi on the backs of black workers, had seen thousands like him before and assumed that he would go south or west like the rest of his kind when he realized there was no place for him. 'Why, the nerve of the man,' they muttered on Vance Street and Jackson Avenue, 'to think that money can buy breeding and class. Why, everyone knows it's Noblesse Oblige and for genealogical aristocrats like us,' they'd say as the men let tobacco spittle saturate their beards and the women picked their noses.*"

"Ah, I-don't-want-to-hear-this-shit-ok?"

"*But Winchester didn't give a damn about all of that. He was there to forge himself a birthright by building the biggest house, growing the most and best cotton, and marrying the whitest, most English- or Dutch-stock Vance or Adams Street woman he could find. Like most Europeans and Africans in the new world, he was a little bit of everything, but he clung to the story that he was from Wales, even when the Irish brogue belched out at parties, the German 'd' endings burped forth at the opera house, and the Elizabethan/Afro 'be' progressive verb tenses drunkenly oozed out as he entertained on his massive porch. Why, the man was positively American.*"

Zip was sitting, straddling a chair; he began to slowly push himself in the chair backward toward the corner. For each inch he backed away, Johnston, on his knees with a hand full of notes and photocopies, bounced forward.

"*Where the gold came from, the self-appointed genteel of Memphis pretended they never knew, and Winchester paid gold up-front for everything, no matter how outrageously overpriced the local merchants marked up their wares in their attempts to run him out. There were veranda whispers of a Federal gold train robbery that had occurred to the north 2 years before; mint-julep gossip of diamonds smuggled in from the Argentine and into New Orleans resting comfortably in Winchester's stomach, then shat out and traded for gold; simple*" *swill ravings about the sale of his family's dilapidated estate in Wales. But only Winchester himself knew of the unspeakable and sardonic slave deals he had master-minded— only Winchester and the 106 male and female slaves he had brought with him from nowhere.*

"After L'Ouverture's successful revolt in Saint-Dominique in 1801, white slave-owners in the Caribbean and on the U.S. mainland complained that every 'nigger' in the Gulf had a bad attitude. You know how it is with people. They see some of their kind make a success of themselves, and they get the notion that they can do it too. You shoulda seen the state blacks had us in before the Mameluke rebellion in A.D. 1270. Well, anyway, slaves in the Caribbean, Florida, Alabama, Louisiana— all over down there— they started thinking 'If Toussaint can do it in Haiti to the French, people with a for-real decadent aristocracy and monarchy and snuff in little gold boxes behind them, well we can certainly run off this European trash that's beatin us and brandin us and makin us eat fish heads for sustenance.' Blacks started fightin with over-seers, cussin atem, talkin back, tellin them how their white ancestors were still tryin to figure out how to cook their meat without burnin their hands while at the same time in lower Egypt, Khafre was just finishing up the architectural wonder of the gigantic replica of his broad nose, forehead and lips on the head of a stone, sanctified lion-man— a Sphinx they called it; y'know, the slaves were just generally being fresh.

Of course, these slaves were immediately throttled, had their tongues snatched out; they were skewered on large sticks; and sometimes the slavers would tie several wild cats to the neck of a bound slave and aggravate the cats til they scratched and tore the slave to death, and other quaint Southern customs like that, but the owners couldn't kill all of them; you couldn't throw good money away like that. I mean, who would clean up the horse shit and pour the tea? But all of the blacks now had a bad attitude, thinking they were as good as whites and stuff.

And the kids they were poppin out were even worse, thinkin that the lack of a bloody past on their hands made them even better than whites. Then this bad attitude started spreading up the east coast and the Mississippi."

Zip searched in his pockets for his old scout knife, sighing when he realized it was in his regular clothes— not his satin performance jumpsuit.

"And at the height of this problem, oh around 1830, who washes up on Key West from a sunken slave ship but Millbranch Winchester, and having been bugged all his life by rich whites, he smells right away the opportunity to undo dispossessed blacks, so much like himself, and become one of those he despised.

Y'know, the worst things that ever happen to the oppressed are always done to them by each other.

"Genocide through murder, miscegenation, and the purposeful dissolution of family units was nothing new to the world by 1831. It's just that they call the 19th-century an age of refinement and science in the history books, and it's just a little bit shocking to a person like me when I go through these old records and ledgers and things that no one else seems to pay any attention to and come across this sort of blood-curdling shit. And I woulda still been killin myself for students and scholarship for less money per year than it would take a zombie to live on if I hadn't found what I found.

"Winchester wanted not only immense amounts of gold to franchise his Murder Inc. plan from plantation to plantation and state to state, he wanted certain hand-picked slaves, young ones he could train, to be given to him gratis. And he was given whatever he wanted. He was credited with bringing stability and order to Civilization. And in some of the plantation diaries it's asserted that in the twenty years it took to cool out black-equality notions, Winchester became the richest man in the New World."

Zip looked up longingly toward the window— bars!

"Oh, who knows, but in 1858 he paid gold for a ship and he put his 6 hand-picked slaves he'd raised and trained on it and they sailed back to somewhere in West Africa, and in 1859 two ships registered as being owned outright by Winchester put in port at New Orleans. Winchester had the blacks chase off the customs officials the first day, but when they came back with an armed militia on the next morning, Winchester ran down the gangway and hugged them, gave the customs officials Dahomey coffee and Nigerian sweets, gave the militia Togo wine, had the half-dozen remaining blacks sing "Old Man River." Oh it was a party! They didn't even want to inspect the ships after that, but Winchester insisted.

"But there was nothing in the ships but a few casks of wine and some foodstuffs. Winchester asserted that he'd been carrying slaves that he'd already sent ashore the night before, but there were slave-holds in only one of the ships. That ship had regular sleeping quarters and slave racks below deck, but the other ship was hollowed out in the hold to make one large chamber, and its floor was savagely scratched with deep grooves, as though something enormously heavy had been pushed or dragged to the hold opening and then hoisted out.

"When he got to Memphis in 1859 he was met by the rest of his slaves at the landing, and they escorted him straight to the land registry office where he

bought 40 acres of land out east, beyond what was then the boundary of the city.
As far as I can tell by cross-referencing maps, what's left of it is still somewhere in
the Chickasaw Gardens/Cherokee Park part of town in Memphis today— bout
a half-mile of woods and secrets left that hasn't been built over. But I gotta go to
Memphis again and check it for sure. "

Usually a knee to the chin stuns anyone long enough for you to get away.
"If only I can hit him so he doesn't block the door with his dead weight," Zip
thought.

"For a while they wouldn't even attend his parties on that beautiful acreage,
but then the rumors of war started, and a white man was a white man— at
least that's what the big whites told the little whites when the big whites saw their
estates and privileged way of life endangered. So the Boys got chummier. Still,
they wouldn't give up one of their daughters to him.

"When the war started, Winchester was sure that the one way of cementing
acceptance after the South had won was to fight— well, at least to enlist, wear
a uniform, pay to have some rank bestowed on him for donating some gold to
Lee, and then, surely, after they'd turned D.C. and NYC into bushlands, one of
the families from downtown or on Peabody Ave. would let him impregnate one
of their daughters and that would be that. Real brandy from France and enough
black women tied-down and gagged out back of the big house to satisfy even
Thomas Jefferson would be the tune he danced to til he died. But y'know how
REAL LIFE is: it never conforms to the notion of history we'd prefer to believe.
War came. The South was gettin slam-dunked everywhere, and when Winchester
was told in 1863 at his observation tent, located at the top of a hill at the back of
yet another losing battle at Nashville, that Memphis had fallen, he made tracks
for home. Things being what they were and him being what he was, it took him
til 1864 to get home, by which time he realized that the writing was on the wall
for the South; its day was done as a world power, and from then on it'd have to
rewrite the past and whine about the present.

"Winchester's slaves were freed when the Feds came in, but the slaves
wouldn't leave Memphis, cause they knew he'd be back as soon as he had heard
what happened, and they still didn't know which side would win the war. Better
to be good to old and new whites than takin a chance on choosing the wrong side.
When he crawled into one of the rear cabins, stinking, sick, and tired, they greeted
him, hugged him, 10 or 20 of the young ones looking like swarthy-faced versions
of him, but when they greeted him they stood over him and looked him straight

in the eye. And that's when he knew that the very battle he'd fought and won for
other whites he couldn't stomach in the first place, he'd lost on his own land, and
here these blacks were— his blacks!— back to their old equal selves again. Hard
to understand blacks... Carlyle called blacks 'amiable blockheads' who were the
only people in the world who could live among whites and not be killed off. Lord
knows, in the last 2,000 years every possible thing has been tried to kill us, er, I
mean, them off, and they keep multiplying and retreatin to the drums.

"Other than helping him get safely out of Memphis he had `one last
request' of them he begged: would they burn down that grand house and all the
surrounding structures on the property? — I think to conceal the secret that his
6, now gone, had crafted and he had hidden, along with their help, whom I think
he'd killed after they helped him bury what they and others like them had made
it possible for him to acquire.

"Mrs. Burnett-Jones believes that the... whatever it was, jewels, gold coins,
had been gathered and buried somewhere else, all together, from its original 30 or
40 marked places around the plantation. No one would have any reason to come
to that spot if everything useful in the area were destroyed, don't you see? But I
don't know if she's right, and she, herself, says that it's just a guess handed down
to her from her mother.

"Well anyway, according to this diary of Lucinda Jones— one of the
grand-daughters of one of Winchester's former slaves, who taught herself to read
and write, and the source I got most of this stuff from and whose diary I found
in the bottom of a vat in the Emory library archives— Lord only knows how it
got there— the slaves burned the house. But before Winchester could get back
to get the... stuff, wherever it was, some stupid Federal artillery unit overshot
the battlelines at Richmond by 300 yards and dropped a fragmentation shell
on his observation tent. All that was left of Major Millbranch Winchester was
a gold tooth and one boot. But according to Mrs. Jones, Winchester had always
anticipated that he might need to hide that gold in a crisis and send his slaves for
it. And that's weird cause evil people seldom believe in physical retribution in this
life, much less spiritual retribution. But he hid a map of his buried-treasure spot
anyway in a place no one would have any reason to suspect a map— at least
that's my guess."

"Well, ah, where's that old dude?"

Zip had backed his chair as far away from this crazy man and his
drug-story as he could. Obviously, this old boy had been eating straight
methamphetamine and might explode in a fury of red and busted dreams

any second. Zip thought if he humored him he'd finish his story and leave him alone.

"Why me? Zip thought. "Why between every set do I have to attract at least one nut to my dressing room? I knew I shouldna sung that Diana Ross song. Um axin 'I'm Comin Out' from my show forever."

Dennis got off his knees and sat up straight against the back of a chair facing Zip.

"It's encoded. It's gotta be coded some kinda way onto the original blue-prints of the house and no one has ever had any reason to look at those plans until now. Doesn't that make sense? Winchester wasn't worried about getting anything of his out of the big house; the Yankees could have it or it could all be burned up. He didn't give a damn. That means that wherever the directions to the treasure were, they whadn't in that house. So they've got to be on the structural plans— which have stayed nice and safe in the land registry office and later in the Memphis Public Library for over a 150 years!"

"Fine, why don't you just go to Memphis and find these plans and get rich and leave me the fuck alone? I got a show to do in 3 minutes and you ain't even given me time to piss. Did you see that woman you slammed my door on when you strong-armed your way through the crowd in the hall? That was Alicia Keys! ALICIA KEYS! Man you *must* be crazy."

"Um not crazy, and I'll never get to see those plans without you. You and me we're going 50-50. You gotta come to Memphis with me."

"Man you're crazy! Help! Help! Somebody ! There's a crazy man in my dressing room! Help! Murder! Rape!"

Dennis grabbed Zip and tried to wrestle him to the floor, but Zip was too solid. He pushed Dennis down and bolted for the door. Dennis grabbed an ankle and bit into it as hard as he could.

"Oww! You're insane! Leave me alone! Help!"

When Zip raised the bitten ankle to look at it, Dennis knocked the other leg from beneath him.

"Oww! Shit. Cut that out now! I don't care if you are retarded, I'll beat your ass. Help!" Zip pounded on the bottom of the grimy door, but his fans in the hall were too loudly discussing him as an obsession for his screams to be heard.

Quickly climbing on top of the fallen Angel, Dennis pleaded.

"Look, please, listen to me. I know it all sounds crazy, but it's true. I know it's true. It-It's … got to be true. And nobody can get to those plans but a family member! Listen to me!"

"Fine, fine" Zip yelped, "but what's that got to do with me— oh no, don't tell me. Um not like onea them *Roots* descendants and you've found my white Kunta? Don't tell me that. I don't wanna know. The past is dead. Only the present and the future's important. Lord, why do I attract the psychos? Maybe it's my cologne."

"Right right, you're onea them slaves' descendants and I can prove it. Goddamit listen to me. We're gonna be ri— "

Zip rolled Dennis over hard onto the door.

"You're on Zip honey. Get your ass out here fo these women tear up the club. Zip! You in there?"

"Peggy! Help! I'm trapped in here with Charles Manson's son.

"Zip? Zip? Say something. Are you in the bathroom? Zip?" screamed Peggy.

Outside the locked dressing-room door, Zip could hear the usual night-chant as he struggled to subdue this madman who had memorized the riffs of every Coleman Hawkins' solo, but who obviously couldn't afford to replace a 15-year-old tweed jacket.

"WE WANT ZIP!
HE CAN SHOOT IT FROM THE HIPS!
WE WANT ZIP!
HE CAN SHOOT IT FROM THE HIPS!
WE WANT ZIP—"

Trying to hang onto Zip's chest and hold his arms down, Dennis blurted,

"Zip, does the name Alice Burnett mean anything to you? It's your great-great-grandmother's name, right? How would I know that? What about Esther Burnett? Why would I wanna know that? Why would I give a damn about your folks when I don't even know you?"

"Because you're insane. Let me go fool!"

"How about Louis Jones? Huh? Ring a bell, asshole? Zip, I tracked you down through them. I traced them back to Winchester's plantation. Zip, it's you I tell you. You're the one. Your folks in Memphis won't let me in the door. Had me arrested for trespassing."

Zip stopped struggling.

"You actually went to my folks' house? Man you're lucky to be alive. Are you for real?"

"Zip... um as real as that treasure. All we got to do is go get it."

"Memphis is on my shit list right now."

"Wealth is god. God forgives all things. Winchester knew that. I can look in your eyes and tell you know it too. You and I, we're the same."

Sitting up and breathing hard, Zip looked the crazy man right in his pale blue eyes. The right word always got Zip's attention.

"But why do you need a family member to see some old plans? Who cares if you go in there by yourself or with a brass band?"

"They're in an exclusive research room in the Memphis public library. You practically have to go in there nude with your head bowed down to see any of the stuff. I couldn't get past the muscular matron at the door. But you, you're family. I can prove it on paper, and nobody but family can see the rare stuff before 1900. They assume all the records have to do with the *white* descendants of DisneyWorld, and the family members would leave the bad stuff in their memories and not pollute the lies of the past with the truth in the present. All you got to do is go in there and sneak some photos. We'll blowem up and figure it out from there."

"Allrightallrightallright. I'll go I'll go! Alice Burnett huh? Mama used to drag out that old Bible with all those faded names to make me memorize'em and make me know myself

... just let me finish the second show. Then we'll get in your car and head for I-40."

"WE WANT ZIP.
HE CAN SHOOT IT FROM THE HIPS..."

"I... I don't own a car right now. My '72 Granville Pontiac played out while I was in Memphis." Dennis looked down and straightened his clothes. "I'm just a college English professor you know. No need to embarrass me. What about your car?"

"Sold it to a finance company for the cash to get a synclavier for the act. I've almost got enough saved now to get it back, but I don't have it right now."

"Well, looks like we ride that Dog."

"You got that right. And *you* goddamit pay for the tickets Prof. Johnston. Now I must be crazy. But I could stand to see my parents. Haven't seenem in over two years. I gotta **DONNEL** these people down and then we can head out. Damn. Look what you done done. Where's my floppy with the charts on it?"

* * *

17

where he was killed in valiant action leading his men against insurmountable Union odds at the Battle of Atlanta.

Once again we can see how the European-money-backed, treacherous, mongrel YANKEES used repeating weapons, superior German cannon, white-hating escaped slave recruits, feces infected, free-floating water systems, mortars, 8-month entrenchment and horrible starvation that forced the Women and CHILDREN of Atlanta to eat horses, their pets, rats, and eventually each other, in their simple and valiant attempt to salvage their beautiful way of life from the hands of white, Yankee Carpet-Baggers and black Nationalists who had hated whites ever since they had been brought to our beautiful country.

The South had invented a way of life that produced culture and architecture the likes of which this world had never seen before. Major Winchester's own homestead, affectionately called "STORM HAVEN" by those who marveled at its beauty, was itself an example of the beautiful and unique art and architecture of, this, NO FAIRER LAND.

The old Winchester Plantation was said to be on a par with the magnificent Hanley Plantation of antebellum Memphis.

Siedah closed the history of Memphis reference book.

"Well, there's nothing odd here that would indicate why they wouldn't let me see those plans today. There's nothing secretive or spectacular or 'valiant' here in this book. It's a standard, boring, candy-coated bio of a Confederate land- and slave-owner. What does she mean, a family member!? To see some fucking antiquated plans for 10 minutes? What's the big deal? Lord, what am I gonna tell the company? That restauranteur is shelling out big bucks to us to come up with the exact replica of this Winchester house, and I'll be damned if I'll be defeated by some hairy woman with biceps as big as my head."

She looked back at the matron behind the desk who had her arms folded and seemed to be standing at attention.

"I'll call Jim, explain the situation. Get him to call the head of the library, and then by having one white person talk to another, maybe I'll be allowed to do my fucking job."

She smoothed her Ellen Tracy suit and looked out onto McLean Street as two Pharaohs' sons jogged north toward Overton Park.

"I'm making that call now and let them handle it. The machine'll pick up the return message. I'm getting out my joggin suit and get me some… exercise."

* * *

Earlier that morning, a BlackDog express bus had pulled out from Atlanta headed northwest.

Chapter 8

"U-h-h-h... Lord God where am I this time?"

Millbranch Winchester (for such was the name he'd given himself, while at the same time promising never to remember his real name again), raised his cut, battered body up from the waves to see cypress trees as far as his salt-weakened vision would take his scan.

"Goddam I'll never understand those people as long as I live I swear to god... they, they'd rather take the ship down—the whole ship, white men, the stolen gold, them chained to the middle deck, everything—down to the coral reef than set foot on this continent as alive-and-well slaves. Even after I tried to explain to'em that we were takin'em to a traditional African form of slavery, where they would be accepted into the tribe and later be allowed to mate with tribal members so that their offspring would become a part of the European tribe... for some reason they just didn't buy that shit. But um the best liar ever born and their craniums are only supposed to be half as big as ours, least that's what Carlyle wrote. I never will understand those people.

"If they had come up like I did... understood what it meant to be *real* dirt, bird do-do. To be a part of that new, white Civilization—with all the guns so that we could re-write history past the year A.D. 1000 and ignore all that mumbo jumbo nigger dominance before that—to be a part of that crowd and still be spat on because you just simply couldn't buy class—at least not in your own life-time; you could buy class for your children if you got rich enough, but you could never have it for yourself if you came from what I was. Then they'd understand that we were offerin'em a good deal. Why, in a 1,000 or so more years, they could just hang around and interbreed and by osmosis get all the stuff that um havin to kill 20 or 30 white men and 2 or 3 thousand niggers to get. I tell you, those people don't appreciate nothin and they don't trust *nobody*.

"Hell, I know um nothin now, but the reason um gonna be somethin is I made two right moves in my whole life—I mean, besides the big move of gettin away from that white trash loser family of mine. Fuck`em I say. If you're white in this world of 1830, in this land of promise, you ain't got but one excuse not to be rich and that's if you're deadern Tarharka's nuts. Anyway, I did two things right: I got a job doing all the nigger work for the richest white man in Richmond, a man with a library so big and so comprehensive that it mighta rivaled that one we burned down in Alexandria, and I learned to read. And what I read was all history—tampered-with history of course, but since we was the ones doing the tamperin, I could read between the lines.

"And that's how I knew about the niggers and what they had been once and it's what's gonna help me subdue'em now. Arrogant bastards. Over there in Mëroé, Nubia, and Kush laughing their asses off at the white savages they'd capture when they sailed out into the Mediterranean to establish new spice or mining colonies. Putting us in cages like monkeys and taking us around the villages and cities in Khmt (we changed that one into "Egypt," a word that has no historical existence before "aigyptos," an ill-thought-out Alexandrine Greek anagram (330 B.C.) for Menes' second crown city, Ineb-hedj, (Hikuptah) (Memphis), that signified the entire topography of what early Greeks called "The Land of the Blacks," which is what "Khmt" [we changed that one to 'Chem' in the Bible] meant in the first place; shit, "Egypt" was an act of sheer genius, you can't even trace the etymology of that one in Dr. Johnson's dictionary), down into Nowe, later No-Amon (we changed that one to Thebes), down into Kush (we changed that one to the Sudan), Axum (we changed that one to Ethiopia, later Abyssinia), into Abu Simbel (the Arabs changed that one so long ago *I* couldn't even figure out what it was originally), even over into Punt (we changed that one into Somalia). Hell, could we help it that we were 3,000 years behind civilized people? You'd think the strong would wanna bear the infirmities of the weak, but no, all they could do was laugh at us cause we had no history and, thus, no **ka**.

"And we knew, we knew right then even before the 1st of 25 Dynasties that spanned another 3,000 years—Menes, (we changed that one to Narmer) that arrogant cocksucking, scum-eating Nubian started everything—uniting upper and lower Khmt—that if we ever got the chance, we'd pay those black bastards back for being so fucking superior. Hell, they wouldn't even let us in their countries, much less into the best schools in the world. How were we supposed to advance? Segregationist slime! And then they'd turn right around and call us dumb when they wouldn't make education available for everyone, knowing all the time we couldn't afford it.

"And those few of us who did manage to sneak onto the grounds of the universities and temples to take the entrance exams would fail because the damn tests were so black-oriented. Hell, how were we supposed to answer socially-based, socially-biased measurements of "intelligence" when every question was black civilization-based and the blacks had purposely kept us out of their civilization? That's just not fair.

"Hell, but they got tired. Sustaining a civilization that kicks the shit outta everyone else for 6,000 years is a bit exhausting. And plus they were so **ARROGANT**! Anybody over in Africa woulda bet you a million gold shekels to one that whites would never even learn to walk up-right.

"Yeah, but we did you snotty bastards. When the Semites figured out that the blacks were a matriarchal people, we let them do the dirty work for us. That black pussy was hard to get—the blacks made the Semites wait 300 years outside the outskirts of Fostat (we changed that one to Cairo) before they'd even let'em into the city, and you have to figure they'd have to wait another generation or so before they could impregnate the lowest class of black women and then another generation or so before the kids could move up in the class structure, and the another generation or so before their kids could do some magnanimous deed and get noticed by one of the Pharaohs enough to be invited to the royal court. But they got in, that's the point. By the time we got there in force with Alexander, the blacks didn't know who they were and they were so tired of being the best that they didn't even care; completely preserved cities under hundreds of tons of sand, and nobody gave a damn. And so with the help of the Arabs we undid their history, we made it so they didn't have none, and so they were through. Arrogant bastards.

"And so I learned two things from all them books, just before I put arsenic in the old man's tea, raped his wife and daughters—snooty bitches, callin me by my first name and shit—and shipped out on the first slave ship I could sign up on: first, you must constantly keep the niggers down by un-writing "history" (what was that Napoleon called history, "a set of lies agreed upon"?) or they will remember what they were once and that'll be our asses. It's a goddamned biological imperative um tellin you. Look how vindictive we were when we finally got the chance, and hell, the blacks didn't even want no land that wasn't in Africa. Think of what they'll do to us for undo'em. We'll end up just like the Galibi (we changed them to Indians), nothin but a bunch of empty mansions in Vicksburg and some faded daguerreotypes of ugly people who no longer exist.

"And secondly, it's not enough to cut off the nuts, rip out the hymens, and cut off the feet of a people to keep'em down. You gotta get to their minds. And the easiest way to do that is convince them that there ain't no history but yours, and you gotta makem learn your set-of-lies-agreed-upon. Pretty soon, you can convince them they ain't got no minds. And then they're yours.

"And boy I can feel it right now that the time is perfect for what I got in mind. Those dumb limeys over in Britain kinda slowed me down by abolishin slavery there a coupla years ago, but we just signed that Indian Removal Act in this country this year, so I know the government and the people down here will go for what I got in mind.

"I say we get to these savages' minds by showing them that we ain't got no heart. I say we beat, we cut, we torture, and we maim every nigger from Boston to Barbados. I say we beat the living shit out of men, women, and children—especially children, gettem started out the right way. I say we work'em from sun up to sun down, feed'em corn-tack and water, make'em fuck for two or three comes in 15 minutes to get more living capital, and then wakem up again at sun-up and puttem to work. I say we never leavem alone; when we see'em we always askem where they goin and where they been. I say we teachem only the right parts of the Old Testament (we stole that one from Ikhneton's [Amenhotep IV] "Articles of Faith) so they'll know what good slaves are supposed to be. Promise'em some milk and honey and some shoes to walk around in when they're dead and they'll live only to die.

"We have to do it and do it now, and I think I can sell my plan to the white scum who've over-run this beautiful continent, cause they'll do anything to keep it cause they remember what *they* were once. Maybe I'll show up on the doorstep of some rich young punk in Mobile. I'll be carrying a dozen or so severed nigger heads with flies on'em, and when they open the door, I'll spit and I'll say, 'I heard chall been havin some trouble down here. This is the way I handle trouble,' and then I'll take a big bite outta onea them heads.

"Ha! Man, after that, news'll spread to Pensacola, Gulfport, and then up the river and out into the Gulf that the Saviour is back and he ain't takin no black names. I'll hire me a crew of depraved trash almost as blood-thirsty as I am and that'll be that.

"And every time I lop off a head or ram a hot iron up some black ass, I'll see that fat-bellied, numb-nutted, swill-drinking snotty British-derived bastard in Richmond. And every time I shoot off some nipples or sew some pussy lips closed, I'll see the Three Whores of Babylon who thought they were too good to blow their noses on me, and I'll laugh and I'll laugh and I'll laugh. And then I'll kick some more black ass, and the rich white bastards will pay me. And then my children can look down on other white children who ain't got as much money, and the lies-agreed-upon will make me a hero.

"And then I'll get me a ship and a good nigger crew—I can't chance takin no jealous white trash along—and I'll go to Nigeria (we changed that one from Yorubaland) and I'll get what I know *has* to be there.

When Tarharka saw the weak rulers to come after him and the growing threat of that damned desert to the North, the Assyrians to the east, and the Libyans to the west, he knew that if there were to be *African* dynasties after his death, the object that carried the **ka** and **Ma'at** of every EgyptianNubianKushiteEthiop had to be protected and hidden, the power of Amon ("The Hidden One") had to manifest itself in the saving of the object.

"At the height of his power in 630 B.C., Tarharka dispatched two full divisions of his best fighting men, 2000 chariots and wagons of scholars, historians, teachers, and priests, three of his own six daughters ("The Sacred Virgins of Aset") and three of his own six sons ("Pharaohs: The Gods Who Walk as Men"), to go southwest from his southern capital at Thebes (we had to change that one again to 'Zoan;' the bastards made Thebes as black as Nowe) on a journey from which they would not be allowed to return. They were to travel southwest until they came to "the green, fertile, land of Nok," and there they were to establish the XXVI-th-B Dynasty and not look back. With them they would take the living fonts from which all of West Africa sprang—that is, themselves—and the "emblem-that-was-all-of-themselves-that-they-could-not-see" and all that their corporeal bodies could not contain.

"Herodotus, the biggest liar in history except for Belzoni, writes that when Tarharka had the top of **IT** excavated and pried from the center mall of the Temple of Amon at his northern capital in Tanis, all of EgyptNubiaKushEthiopia cried out collectively, and Tarharka's apparent successors decried him as a mad-man and a heretic.

"I can hear that arrogant over-educated nigger Tarharka now, 'Oh, it was ok for that fool Ikhneton to start all that one-god-Aton shit that led to the Civil Wars of Monotheism that almost destroyed our empire; that was ok. Punks like you didn't say nothin then. Ran back to your provinces and let the army and the priests fight it out, then came sniveling up after Ikhneton's death and backed the winners, the priests. But let me try to do something that will always preserve the knowledge of us against the barbarians all around us—let someone be the least bit different or show the least bit of back-bone—and you wanna grab your dicks and pull your swords. Punks. I thank Asar when I die I'll never have to see you weak-asses again cause you'll never pass **The Negative Confessions**. Your asses will be forever stuck in the dirt of this world and that's all you deserve. Get outta my sight before I bury you alive. **HOOOEEEEEEBRRRTTTT!**)'"

"But Herodotus gave me enough detail to know where they went, and that's all I need to know. Nok (we changed it to Nod in the Old Testament and kicked all our psychopaths over there, especially Cain) later became Hausaland, became the Songhai Empire, became Yorubaland, became Nigeria. And if **IT'S** in Nigeria, I'll find **IT** and I'll bring **IT** back or die.

"Then let'em see who Millbranch Winchester is. Then they'll know that I'm as white as they. Then they'll know that Millbranch Winchester knows what time it is."

He looked north, ignoring the bloated, floating dead bodies washing up around him, and he began to walk, tripping over his own feet. 150 miles (240 kilometers) of hopped, skipped, and swum Keys later, and he'd knock someone in the head, take his horse, and ride into Miami.

He was on his way.

Chapter 9

"I was feelin so good, everything goin so right, and then I get unstuck with this freak. What am I doin here, headin west again?"

Outside the tinted window of the Dog, Zip's darkened reflection stared back at his tux shirt and untied bow. Over his reflected left shoulder, he could see Dennis, out completely, dreaming who-knew-what lunatic dreams.

The light-blue of the tux shirt refracted and multiplied as the first rays of diffused sunlight seeped through the gray dawn clouds. The blue covered Zip's face, Dennis, the aisle, the adjacent passengers, hit the opposite window and bounced back onto Zip. He was completely tangled.

"What coulda been better? Makin money at something you love, gets you women, and keeps you outta a lotta **CS** cause itsa artistic domain the Fans have conceded to the Afros— for the minute. Mr. Hugh… nobody walks out on Mr. Hugh. Mr. Hugh'll never take me back. Took it kinda personal, too, like I was walkin out on Peggy. But we weren't only potential sex-mates, we're friends too, and she understands that I'll never be satisfied til I get what I want—if I can ever figure out what that is.

"Plus, stuff was gettin too hot, and I saw L-O-V-E about to pop up on the CRT for both of us. Then what would we have done? I definitely woulda hurt her feelings cause I ain't never had enough of nothing, and what was she gonna do with that head-knocker of a boyfriend she's had for years? Tellim 'Baby, this is Zip and we've been humpin like hounds for two years, and I want you two to shake hands and come out lovin each other. It's ok Zip honey. I'll keep FIST locked in the opposite bedroom and throw him a live chicken every mornin. He'll understand. Here, rub his belly; he likes that.' Naw, just wouldna worked. That man's stuck in the '80s."

"But I will be back. And if I could come back to Hot 'Lanta rich… I learned a lot about Atlanta though. It wasn't what I thought it would be… what all the ads in the black magazines say it is. Me, of all people, believing in heaven-on-earth. Nigger Heaven. Just stupid, naive, that's all I am, at my age. Thinkin that from the hearts and minds of the Diasporic Original People here in the states would spring some kinda moral megalopolis with honorable people pushing the buttons and cuttin the checks. Polite and fair to everybody, but don't have to answer to nobody negative if they don't want to.

"Shit, I musta been crazy. I know money don't work that way. Money chooses who it wants for public relations purposes and starts pushing the audio and video buttons to manufacture the illusion. Of course, the blacks in the puppet-show convince themselves that they're autonomous, when they're really just automatons. That's when they become Complete Fools; they're just level-1 fools as long as they think they're deceiving others about their real status in the system, but when they deceive themselves that they're important, that's when they can have their plugs pulled the easiest. And there's nothing sadder than a nigger outta work who thought he was important enough to speak his mind. But I guess believing those illusions, grinning up the green, is better than being doped-up and outta work. It's all so complicated.

"All I know is the blacks downtown in the suits don't want nothin to do with them blacks across the expressway in the hospital shirts and ShopMart sweats. And these upwardly-mobile blacks is some weird cut-throat, black-back-stabbing motherfuckers. If you waved your hand over their heads, you'd bump into all them white strings.

"And the farther up the ladder they go, the more bizarre they get. They laugh in the church basement at traditional religion and blow their noses at Vodun, but the shit they do believe in is like a caine addict's DTs. This one here goes to the same psychic as the "best" white millionaires in her town go to before she makes a business decision; that one over there gets his leaves read before he'll have sex with his wife; this other one combines Scientology with Jehovah's Witnesscism and comes up with, I don't know, I guess he's a scientific witness for Jehovah before he jacks-off quietly in his law office and steals another poor black's house for 20 g's under market value.

"I'd go in a bar or a club, and I'd have to conduct a search for a black Georgian. Everybody was from NYC or D.C. Don't nobody even live in Atlanta; they're all outside I-285, except for the 35 crack babies left per day on the steps of Grady Hospital. But I understand, black Southerners runnin off; Memphians runnin to Atlanta, Atlanteans runnin off to Memphis, New Orleaneans runnin off to Atlanta, everybody runnin to Miami and runnin right back out again. How can you live your whole life and *not* believe that there's somewhere in your own country where people who look like you are treated better? Nope, sometimes illusions, if you believem hard enough, are all that matters, and you can make it on the strength of your own self-deceit.

"A lotta good stuff about Atlanta though. It's a 24 hour town— as long as you stay downtown in the hotels, and there're enough urban types to make it comfortable. You can see other blacks with some degree of control over their own incomes— as long as you stay in Atlanta proper. And even though it's surrounded by outposts of Barbaria, it's still the South, and you know it's yours.

"Next week I was gonna move up to UPTOWN ATLANTA, $750 a week and all the Spelman nouveau-riche women I could stand. Now, look at me, headin west, but at least um stoppin 1 bridge short of No Blacks Land. Before I realized that one-page pieces of writing that ain't set to music in this century are a goddamed waste of ink that nobody pays for, I wrote a poem about all that hostile space west of the river once. How'd it go now?"

* * *

West of the River

the Indians stay out of downtown.
The Mexicans multiply and wait.
The whites look right through you—
unless you're wearing a sports uniform
or a waiter's jacket.
And the blacks look for each other in shopping malls
and go to church a great deal.

I was told there are a number of states
west of the river,
but I saw only one vast plain and corn field,
and was subjected to only one philosophy.

I read there was a westward black migration after 1876,
but they must have turned around
and gone back to Jackson;
they couldn't possibly have liked the... climate.

Take my word for it:
Between Memphis and Los Angeles County
there ain't nothing but mean faces,
HEAT,
small businesses founded by his father,

giant oil companies blessed by God,
white boys in business suits who ask if you're the bag boy
at the hotel you're paying $200.00 a night to stay in,
a billion Rev. Billy Bobs,
a man who saw a 900-foot-tall Jesus,
and cowboy hats.
Unless you got to go to the Grand Canyon,
I say skip it.

* * *

In Zip's mind he saw clearly how the map of the United States should be redesigned in the text books. This would be a cartographic-cardiac survival map for non-whites and those whites who were not SleepWalkers or Fans.

Zip agreed with the people west of the Memphis-Arkansas bridge. They *should* be left alone to develop their "culture" and rural ways. They *should* be able to spit phlegm in public forums and clear their air-waves for country music and reruns of The Doris Day Show. People *should* hang out with whom they wanted to hang, as long as they were only hurtin themselves. Why, Zip's demarcation of the country would facilitate individualism—not unlike the ways appraisers, realtors, and banks facilitated individualism when they routinely red-lined neighborhoods.

Those who were human and wanted to live in the present and help prepare for the future of the second half of the 21st-century would be connected to each other by "culture bridges" which would span over more backward areas—principally those areas unurban; the only thing west of the River that would be linked by culture bridges to Chicago, Detroit and Memphis would be L.A.

Whenever anyone civilized wanted to go from one part of the society to the other, they would be perfectly free to do so; but, of course, no one would ever want to leave Civilization to live in "The Heartland." Everybody except the nuts who lived there knew there was no heart in the Heartland.

And once a Myop-Arrogo (an inhabitant of dreaded Ruralia) crossed over to Civilization, it'd have to change its ways and stay in The World. To see a real Myop-Arrogo who refused to change, human beings from Civilization would probably just do as the English did in the 17th-century: visit the zoo on Sundays with the kids and let them laugh at and throw food remnants at the irretrievably insane.

* * *

"Nope, Hot 'Lanta whadnt heaven, but it was better than Memphis. I just appreciated being able to go out and get a sandwich at 2 a.m. that wasn't fast-fried or wrapped in 3-month-old plastic. Something was missing, but it wasn't Atlanta's fault. It was my fault on two counts: believing PR, and needing something else— I don't know what— to go along with my own illusion."

* * *

Zip punched Dennis on the shoulder and pulled his graying beard. The treasure-hunter who once was a scholar roused and looked over at the impetus for his living the last few years.

"Whatta you want now? Goddam you're a pain in the ass. I've never seen anyone fight so hard to keep from being able to pay for maid service. What? What? What is it?" Dennis growled.

"Right, um supposed to get excited about some nut with a pencil-holder in his shirt pocket who tells me he's found **IT** and wants to cut me in on **IT**. You'd think you gays would come up with better lines than that by now. Look, I need someone to talk to, ok? What'd you say you used to do?"

"I was a college professor."

"Well, why'd you give it up? Thatsa a cushy life for you white boys."

"You must get all your economics lessons from the *JET* 'People Are Talking' column, *the* reference source for all you 21st-century educated urban children. You're about as well-informed as my Addidas."

"For your information Mr. William Buckley Jr.-Snob sir, I probably read more books last year than you walked by in the bookstores."

"Do tell? What do you read?"

"Everything. Mostly history of Africa books, Afro-American novels, French and German philosophy—oh, and Harold Robbins of course. I love how all the black dudes in his novels can stay as hard as diamond for a whole month."

"What depressing reading material."

"Yeah, but I spend a lotta time alone at night with Sarah Vaughan on the head-phones to make up for it. College professor huh?"

"Yes, that's right."

"Well, so what happened?"

"It's just a long story you don't wanna hear. I just woke up one day that's all. And then I couldn't do the things I used to do anymore."

"So what did you useta teach?"

"OK, you asked. Well, I started out as a new Ph.D. teaching basic composition. You know, it's kinda like being a new M.D. and being put in the emergency room on Saturday nights in downtown Miami for a coupla years—but much, much bloodier. I was so young and expected so much and the writing was so… Martian. Anyway, I moved "up" from there to teaching business writing. I got burned out on that after realizing those young adults only wanted to know how to write one thing: "Please hire me!" and the employers responded only with jobs that made the kids do every micro-dot of writing the secretaries weren't doing and paid them minimum wage for writing everything from anniversary notes to annual reports. I understand professional writing is a lucrative career choice now, as 'careers' now go, but um talkin about back in the '80's when everyone was still suspicious and jealous of people with pens and a knowledge of semantics.

"Boy, and then I did it. I *really* did it. They'd been offerin me these American literature courses for years, but I knew better: that stuff, the way it was writtin in those canonical books was D-E-A-D, and anybody who taught it would pretty soon have moss growing outta his mouth, too. So, n-o-o-o, I bit the big apple, I decided to teach literary theory. Ha Ha Ha! Boy, by the time *I* figured that garbled shit out, I knew I didn't want to infect any other human beings with it.

"We were at the stage back then when we were denying that the "surface" narrative in front of us, y'know, the story in other words, existed at all, and that, in fact, what was really important was the literary criticism about the narrative that did exist in the hypothesized readers' minds, whose minds by the way did not exist anyway because they were "hypothesized," but even if these minds had existed they wouldn't have been important anyway because the narrative existed for itself, of itself, and in itself, and didn't need no reader no how. God, there was no chicken before the egg. There was just an egg, and it sprouted little feet and walked around and never hatched and what's it to you thank you very much kiss my ass. God, I'd rather be forced to watch reruns of *The Waltons* and *Little House on the Prairie* than read a word of that psycho-babble again.

"I hear it's gotten more human now; they're sayin that what the author intended and what the reader interprets maybe is somewhat important, and that *maybe* there's no way for a literary critic to gauge either thing. The new stuff all comes from France of course. You can bet two things for sure in this life: when a new generation of French boys needs to pay the rent, they'll invent a new 'school' of literary theory that says all the theories before theirs were horse poop. And number 2, you can bet your grand-daddy's last pair of long-drawers that we in the U.S. will buy the do-do, translate it quickly and very poorly, and pass it on to young, ugly, pimply-faced Ph.D.'s with dandruff in their hair and wax running out of their ears. We'll tell them it's the New Gospel According to the Continent. Europhiles that we are, we figure anything that's white, ain't ours, that we don't understand, and that has no relation to our own experience must be pretty good.

"So after Theory Trauma I took my ass back to the basement and composition. How can I put it? I actually felt 'useful.' I was teaching 18-year-olds different ways of expressing themselves on paper, and I was reaching them. Suddenly, the emergency room didn't seem so bad anymore after seeing what really went on up in the wards. And then those people in the caps and gowns put my graying head out on the street for not havin enough current publications.

"When I asked them what did it matter if I were still turning out good writers, they said it mattered cause the State Board of Regents of Georgia said it mattered. I said 'But suppose I don't say anything important or helpful to young writers in my publications, suppose I just grind out theory and speak do-do-ese and get it published through bribery and friends?' And they said, 'Cool, groovy. Then you'd be a scholar.' And they pushed this SBR mandate explanation in front of me that explained and validated everything, and it had no signature or initial, 150 typos, 18 subject/verb disagreements, and 10 fused, fragmented, and comma-spliced sentences in a 2 page document. Then I knew the junkies had taken over the clinic.

"So I took my enormous $8,000 dollar retirement in a lump sum, my desk lamp, and my original 1937 edition of the *Journal of American Folklore* with Zora Neale Hurston's "Hoodoo in America," and I started doing something I'd been thinking about doing ever since I'd stumbled onto the Burnett-Jones manuscript a few months earlier: I started looking for you. Impressed?"

To Dennis' right, Zip's snoring almost drowned out the roar of the monstrous bus motor.

* * *

Late the next night as the Dog dieseled up Union Ave. in Memphis headed for the station, Zip couldn't hear the roar of the ascending DC-9 as it headed for Atlanta. Nor could he hear the shouts of "Damn! Damn! Damn!" from a very frustrated passenger on that night coach.

* * *

"I can't believe this. I-cannot-fucking-believe-this! Not only can I not see the damn plans, I gotta fly to Atlanta to see if the damn plans are in some diary! I'm not a historian goddamit. Um an engineer. Don't we subsidize the damn libraries so the rich and the stupid can enjoy ART? How can a librarian turn down a regional VP for NEGCO? Where's the big payback? 'This world sho done gon crazy' as granny would say. What did I do? Why is my Karma feeding me arsenic? Did I step on a crack on the side-walk? Speak my mind to someone with a higher salary? And of all nights! I was on my way. Ooo, he was so fine!"

Siedah had rushed home from the library earlier that day, thrown on her black-and-white personally initialized Dior running togs, zipped down Poplar in the rented 800ZXX+, checked with the hooker at Poplar and Cleveland to find where the joggers might jog in that part of Memphis, and 2-cylindered into Overton Park.

No time to stretch. Pop on the head-phones and stride east, up the north side of the golf-course past the "Great Public Benefactor's" bronze, evading his steely stare and past the stone muses at his gigantic feet, up the grass lane between the museum and the show houses, through the tulip garden and past the kids' swings, a right across the zoo parking lot and down the bus lane, left through the back lanes and past the north zoo gate, back across the bus lane leading south down more shaded black top, around the giant gazebo, and past the fire station, zooming up the south side of the golf course dodging errant balls and unleashed mutts, a right at the clubhouse and past the art school and onto the main pleasure-green, and, finally, there they were, two massive, Memphian men, hand-carved by Catlett.

No need for Siedah to sweat any further; they were thumping the circle of the green and they'd be back to the south end in a minute.

Casually taking her hair band off to let the layers fall, unzipping and letting drop the jacket, unsnapping and dropping the pants to show the cut-back, black-silk shorts, as the boys rounded the last turn, Siedah Jackson exploded into their little Id-centric worlds in full back-stretch.

"Lawdamercy! Who is that? Main, main, main! Hol up hol up. Don't we need to stop and stretch or something? Mercy!"

But Ken was already sprinting past Earl toward Siedah and pulling up lame, falling in the grass, screaming, right in front of her.

"Oww! My leg my leg. Owwooo! Oh pain, shit, cramps! Oww!"

Siedah was ice cause you have to freeze pain before you dive into the hot tub.

"Just stretch it out. You'll be alright," she said.

She forward stretched and half-mooned Ken into wide-eyed, open-mouthed silence. A left thigh-stretch and then a right even made him forget about the lie he had spasmed. Earl came flying.

"Wait a minute wait a minute! Mam (puff) thatsa (wheeze) married man, mam. He has to be in the house every night at 10 o'clock."

"Yea, and then I get up at 4 a.m. and go home to my wife. Mind yo own damn business Earl. Ooo, Mercy!"

Siedah lightly kicked Ken in the calf. Of course he howled like he'd been hit with a steel pipe.

"Then you deserve to cramp up sucker. Trying to get me in trouble."

And then turning to sport Earl a full frontal view: "You got a wife too?"

"Miss, um as free as the top of your Spandex and twice as tight as the bottom. My name is Earl."

Doing full torso stretches: "I'm Siedah."

"Siedah! Oh I love that! Is that French or Spanish or African or what?"

"Itsa 100% grade-A American, like me. Yall through runnin?"

"Where you wanna run? How far you wanna run?!" they screamed in tandem, Ken jumping to his feet.

"Ken, I want you to run south, just as fast as your cramped-up legs can go, and Earl and I are gonna run north at a slow and easy pace."

"Well fuck you too then. Earl, I guess you can get this Git-It-Girl here to take you home. Um outta here."

"Huh, yeah well, whatever. See you tomorrow," Earl mumbled without looking at Ken, and then, re-focusing his eyes away from Siedah's bow legs that ended in the widest arc of heaven he'd ever encountered and onto the most hazel eyes he'd ever seen, "Do you run out here everyday?"

"I run in New Orleans."

"That's a marathon."

"You're a funny guy."

"Yeah, and I taste good too."

* * *

Some people can take their whole essences with them in two Pierre Cardin briefcases, two Calvin Klein shoulder bags, three Anne Klein overnight-cases, four Bill Blass suitcases, and five Geoffrey Holder hang-up bags. The two rooms on Front St. already looked and felt like Siedah, and she'd only been there a day.

Two little framed Jeanne Moutoussamy-Ashe pix over the sofa, Sony CD/casette on the hardwood floor by the bed, and a Toshiba opti-drive laptop on the massive, mahogany desk. One hundred CDs scattered on the floor by the bed, a Sony hooked up to the rented 19", with copies of Jane Fonda's *Workout Book #17*, R. Martin's *Frank Loyld Wright: Prophet of the Future*, and *Purple Rain* dropped on the floor in front of the TV. Continuous-feed paper spilling out of the briefcase, and everywhere, everywhere, the seducing smell of cinnamon incense.

"Hey, this is great! Look at the lights shining off the river. You got nice toes."

"You a toe man? What else do you do all day with your time?"

"I manage a spa out east."

"Uh. Figures. *'Boys & Girls, made to attract/Golden drops glistening/On the curves of their backs...'*"

"You got a nice voice too."

"I got a lotta nice stuff."

"What do you do?"

"I'm an engineer."

"Yea, I can tell, but I mean, what do you do to make money?"

The cognac was talking for him and the Grand Marnier was singing for her, and she didn't know what was coming after this night. Only tonight.

Cause it was time.

"... so baby drown me with your sweat..."

And then there was the telephone.

* * *

"Lord, lessee. Too many of us with no jobs for me to be complainin I guess. Lessee:

31

LUCINDA BURNETT-JONES was born in Fayette County, Oakland, Tennessee in 1868 [?]. She taught herself to read and write and is purported to be the author of <u>The Strange and True History of an American Family</u> (1922), a published diary thought lost until a faded copy, along with other artifacts and rare books [see DUNBAR, Paul, this vol.], was found among the contents of Jean TOOMER'S steamer trunk in 1989 by this author. Burnett-Jones' work, said by other critics to be the missing literary link between the slave narratives and the autobiographical fiction of Afro-Americans during the HARLEM RENAISSANCE, is a recapitulation of her family's past, traced to her original antebellum ancestors, an obscure Confederate Major named Millbranch Winchester, a slave-owner, and Esther Deaner-Winchester-Burnett, a slave on the Winchester plantation. The single known copy of this work is now in the Special Collections of Emory University in Georgia and has yet to be re-edited and reissued.

Burnett-Jones died of causes unknown in 1925.

Boy, that Trudier Harris can write. Well, I guess it's worth a try. I just don't understand why the client is so adamant about these beam stress points and why my supervisor is spending all of this company money on one project. Why don't we just redesign the support beams and roof? All this for an anachronistic restaurant? DamnDamnDamnDamn the man was fine!"

* * *

"Will you please tell me, mam, and I use that term of respect under protest, what would prove to you that this man standing right here is a living descendant of Major Millbranch Winchester of Memphis?"

"From lookin atim, I don't think *anything* could prove that. Are you on that dope, that Mega-Ice? Cause you seein things that ain't."

"Mam, I have explained to you the family line here, showed you that Winchester had many offspring by black women—some of whom were his own daughters—given you some of their names and traced out the end of some of their branches for you, and traced Mr. Peter's line here back to one Lucinda Burnett-Jones; you have the photocopy of the Fayette County Birth Registry, and you can see who Lucinda Jones' mother was and you've got the photocopy of the 1866 newspaper story where little Alice gave the account of who her father was with her holding a photo ofim! **I-can't-take-you-back-any-farther-cause-there-ain't-no-point-and-I-couldn't-if-I-wanted-to-cause-the-man-had-no-past—he-was-a-self-made-swine.**"

The librarian looked Dennis square in the eye.

"I can't make out the face in that photograph. It's too small and the copy's too bad. Furthermore, everybody knows that Major Winchester was descended from a long line of Welsh aristocrats with a genteel, royal past stretching back thousands of years. Also, you asking me to believe that a white gentleman of noble breeding, an army officer, would have… IMPREGNATED black slave women? Don't make me laugh. Why you wanna see those old plans so badly anyway?"

"None of your goddamed business! Umma scholar on leave! That's how I found the diary that got me these facts. Scholars use libraries! Or didn't your dumb-ass know that!?"

"SHHHS" echoed around the first floor of the library, on whose north window was painted representations of the ancient Khemites, Khufu,

Khafre, Ikhnaton, Nefertari, Ty, Hatshepsut, and the more recent Cleopatra, all black. Obviously a municipal oversight.

("Dennis, that ain't no way to get on this mastodon's good side.) Mam, I apologize for my friend's behavior here. He's over 60. He's under a strain. He was just denied tenure after teachin, publishin, doing community and committee work, makin peanuts and workin like a ... er... nigger for 30 years. He's also under a medical doctor's care— which is an additional life-threatenin risk. What would you like me to do, mam, to prove what he says is true so he could examine this plan, piece of paper, whatever it is?"

"Well, I'll tell you what, if foul-mouth there can leave this library without saying another word to me, and you can bring me a copy of some page of this diary yall talkin bout that proves what he says, then I'll let you and him into the Memphis Room. But I still don't believe any of this."

"But, mam, the diary is in Atlanta— least that's what he told me."

"That ain't my problem. You prove it to me, and yall can get in. Now take foul-mouth here and leave the library. I've bout had enough."

She flexed her arms and dragged a hand through her bottle-blond hair. ("Honestly, these Georgia crackers got no sense of allegiance to the past.")

"NOOO! WE'RE NOT GOING BACK TO ATLANTA!" Dennis screamed. Zip clamped his hands over Dennis' mouth and started pushing him out of the library.

"He's a sick mam. It's his medication. The strong have got to bear the infirmities of the weak you know. Forgivim."

"Mmmphrrh! Uhh!"

"Dennis, shut up. Shut up! Do you want to look at the plans or not?"

The river breeze pushing east on Peabody blew Zip's untied bow from his shirt as he pushed Dennis toward the bus stop.

"Get your hand outta my face. She's crazy! I don't have any money to get back to Atlanta. Jesus H. Christ I can't believe Memphis. It's even more backward than Georgia."

"Every place is the same when you're broke and don't know nobody. The only person you know here is me. Now you listen to me. If all this junk is true, and we're runnin into enough roadblocks to make me believe it might be true, the point is to get to those plans, and it don't matter what we gotta do to get toem. So just swallow hard and let's get back to Atlanta. You got $2 to catch the MATA bus to get back downtown?"

"Man, I don't have two cents left. God, where did my life go wrong?

I know, I know; it was scoring so high on the verbal part of the S.A.T. I shoulda paid more attention to the math part. I coulda been something respectable and stable by now, like an accountant. Be near retirement, make 50 g's a year, have a bald head, a big pot belly, a 4 bedroom brick in Marietta, a dumpy wife, 2.3 kids and a drug and alcohol problem. Oh, I woulda been so… so normal. Wouldn't have to go through these highs and lows for being different than the rest of the herd."

"Wait a minute. Let's hope this light catches this woman with her window down."

The Buick Riviera stopped. And as much as she didn't want to, as much as she wanted to act like she wasn't the kind of woman who noticed hunks standing on street corners, her head turned to see who that voice was coming from.

"Baby, surely our love was meant to last/
Problems come, but you know they always pass./
I fall in love with you over and over again./
I don't care about the problems, just wanna be your man./
Though I know that we've been up and down/
It's only your love baby I always wanna be around./
When you tell me that you just don't know/
And our love may end up on the floor/
I say no, no, no, I won't go./
Baby just stay in love with me and I will show,/
That surely our love was meant to last… /"

"Oh it was huh?"

"You can bet on that Pretty Face. Look …" Zip leaned on the door of the Buick and stuck his head in the car just as the light turned green.

"HONK!"

Dennis backed Zip up: "Man, don't blow that horn like that. Can't you see thatsa library over there? Go round!"

"… you can see I've got a tux on… a dirty tux with no tie, but a tux. And even though I've got a white boy with a beard with me, you can see um not low class. Would you pleeeze give us a lift to the BlackDog bus station? Couldn't you just do that for me?"

"Wel-l-l… will you finish the **DONNEL**?"

"I'll look in your eyes all the way as I sing."

* * *

Ten minutes and an exchanged phone number later, Zip and Dennis stood in the lobby of the bus station. With the advent of sleek, much faster planes and their higher, exclusionary fares, bus stations, once the exemplars of glamorous, urban mass transit in the South, had become the junction-mobiles of the lower classes who couldn't afford to fly. Along with the simple, nice majority of people who took the buses to Chicago, Detroit, Jackson, and Nashville, were also the by-products of urban poverty who hung out at the bus stations to figure out what had gone wrong with their lives, and until they found out, they'd bug the shit out of other people to pass the time.

"Well, whatta we do now?" Dennis asked. "Where are we gonna get round-trip bus fare to Atlanta and back again? Have you thought about eating? I'd like to eat. All I've had in the last 36 hours is that piece of chicken that kid gave us on the bus outside of Cookeville. Also, I hate to bring this to your attention, but you stink. I fear I also stink, and I would like to take a bath and brush my teeth. Why not go back to your parents' house?"

"… my parents…"

* * *

When Zip and Dennis had stepped off the bus earlier that day and hiked from downtown to Zip's parents' house, they were met with hugs, kisses, and spaghetti. At least, this was the initial reception, until the situation turned into the Chicago Cubs on a wet playing field.

"Zip honey, look at you, you're as thin as a rail. Here, put some more spaghetti on that plate," said Carrie. "Ah, who's your friend?"

"Mama, this is Dr. Dennis Johnston formerly of ___ University in Georgia, and besides my wanting to see yall, he's the primary reason that um back in Mempho." Zip dropped a wad of $100 bills tied by a rubber band into his mother's apron pocket without her noticing, and then he sank his head into his mother's spaghetti, being reminded by a mound of pasta what love and loving were all about outside the carnal sphere.

"Well, Dr. Johnston, ain't you the same guy we had taken off our doorstep about a month ago? Why didn't you say you were a friend of Zip's?"

"Call me Dennis Mr. Peters. Frankly, I hadn't even met your son at that point. My research had just traced him here. If I had just gotten a chance to really talk to you—"

"We're supposed let any strange white man with a beard just walk all over our property, right? I didn't mean no harm man, but you gotta admit your approach ain't exactly Presbyterian."

"I know, I know, it's just all these brick walls I've been running into in the past few years; it's all made me very, ah, impatient if you know what I mean."

"Well you call me Lester, Dennis. I can relate to brick walls. Now tell me how you got this boy back home. We'd tried everything and the boy kept saying he didn't wanna face us again until he was it. One time we even called him and his mama put a plate of hot spaghetti up to the receiver and let the aroma waft up. He lied and said he could smell it, but he still wouldn't come home. What'd you do, get him that contract in Vegas or something?"

"Well, what it is Lester is this…"

Zip tried to stop Dennis, knowing that the linear fool would start the whole story over again from the beginning, but spaghetti was in his mouth and he was at his mother's table. So…

* * *

"You get the hell outta my house you crazy fool! I can't believe my son would be dumb enough to even listen to that kinda mumbo jumbo. I musta raised a jackass instead of a man. Um tellin you, you get outta here right now. Interrupting this boy's career so you can have a body guard while you drag your hippy ass all over the woods. Get out!"

"But Lester, it's all tru—"

"That's Mr. Peters to you peckerwood. My god, that's gotta be the craziest shit I ever heard in my life. You been prejudiced by watchin too many of those *Good Times* reruns. All black people ain't dumb enough to listen to do-do like that. Treasure! Lord have mercy. Zip, why are you always so bent on takin chances on things that the worst roulette-junkie in Vegas wouldn't bet a penny on?"

"Well Lester now just wait a minute. Maybe what this man says…" Carrie gazed out the dining room window and tried to remember from that time in our lives when everything makes such a big impression that it all gets lumped together and we don't remember any of it.

"I seem to remember rumors about Lucinda. I never met her unfortunately, but evidently that relative of mine was just as other-worldly as the rest of the family. My mama told me that Lucinda was the deepest person she'd ever known. One time she said she walked in on Lucinda without knockin and Lucinda was speaking some old strange African language to herself that she couldn't possibly have known. Mama said the language didn't seem to have no vowels in it.

"Anyway, mama said that whenever Lucinda would start to talk about slavery time, her voice got real, real, low, and she would close her eyes and start naming all these names in reverse chronological order until she got to around the War, and then she would burst out crying and anybody listening would have to wait a while before she could speak again. And then she'd speak about the unspeakable through her tears and sniffling.

"It was all about people none of us knew we were even descended from, people with strange sounding names with a lot of strange lives attached to'em. And she would say, 'They, the 6, couldn't understand how he could do it to them, not after the way they did for him and protected him. All they ever wanted from that white man was the same kind of protection they provided him when he was nobody. But instead, he undid them.' And then mama said she'd start crying again and they'd have to wait again for Lucinda to keep tracing our line.

"I never did hear what the name of this 'he' was or what it was he was supposed to have done or who 'The 6' were. The story was never finished for me… Lucinda called, but I guess nobody responded. I was so little and I guess mama musta thought that the past ought to stay buried where it was and not be carried into the future. But I did find out one thing completely by accident. I wonder if Dennis could be…"

Carrie got up from the table and reached down into the bottom of the china cabinet. When she drew back both her hands she held a thick, family bible faded from the years it had seen.

Zip knew when the bible came out, things were serious, so he sopped the last bit of tomato paste up with a piece of bread, swallowed, and spoke.

"Pop, I felt the same way you do when I first heard this story. But, if you listen to this man, I don't know. It's just something about him. Um tellin you, he's deep. You of all people. Can't you feel him?"

"I don't feel nothing from him. He ain't sending me nothin and I don't wanna receive nothin from him. Lord have mercy—do you still even have a job in Atlanta? You 33 years old boy and no job!"

Carrie walked between them and sat back down at the table. She put on her bi-focals and slowly lifted the torn and faded cover of the bible from the top of the first page.

"Now let me see if I can find what I thought I remembered. This bible traces our line back to 1866 with Linnie Burnett, Lucinda's younger sister and also Lucinda's aunt. Yall stand up and look at this."

The three men congealed behind Carrie's shoulders, their eyes following the tip of her index finger as it went up columns of names and years, page after page, from the year of Zip's birth, to 1868.

"Carrie, this nut says that the whole story comes from Lucinda through people who had to have been born *before* the War, and you already know our bible don't go back that far. Why are you bothering with this," Lester fumed as Dennis looked back through the living room to make sure the front door was unlocked.

When she got to the lower left corner of the last page of the genealogy, she suddenly slammed the front pages of the bible closed.

"Carrie! Good God be careful! That's all we ever were you're treating like the latest issue of *Essence*. What's wrong with you?" Lester screamed.

Carrie turned to Dennis.

"Dennis," she, pulling out a chair from the table and turning it to face her, "sit down right here where I can see your face."

When he had sat, Carrie held his face in her hands and looked him in the eye without blinking.

"In this book you're supposed to have found that Lucinda was supposed to have written where she was supposed to have told all these secrets, how was this book signed?"

"What do mean? I mean, it has her name on the inside cover. She had it privately printed by Wimmmer Bros. Books in Memphis, 1922."

"That's not what I meant."

"I'm sorry Carrie, I just don't follow you."

"What I'm asking you is was there a signature anywhere in this copy you found? You claimed it was one of Lucinda's personal copies. How do you know that?"

"Oh. There… wasn't a signature, but at the back of the book there were initials in faded purple ink and—"

"Where on the last page?"

"In the lower left-hand corner, and underneath there were—"

"Shhh! Be quiet now. Make the marks you saw on that last page right here on this napkin. Make the letters as close to the original as you can remember. Here's a pen."

Dennis didn't know what this was all about, but at least Carrie's seriously entertaining the tale had quieted Lester down, so he made the marks on the napkin and slid the napkin toward Carrie.

"See, she put her initials at the back on the last page, LBJ, inside a triangle, and underneath the initials were the representative hieroglyphs for those consonants. See?"

Carrie stared at the markings on the napkin for a moment and then sighed. But it was a sign of relief, not of anguish. The circle, thanks to Dennis, remained unbroken.

"Mama, what is it?"

Carrie reopened the bible to the last page of the genealogy where she'd kept her finger placed. She pointed to the lower left-hand corner. The same marks.

"See, Lucinda started this bible, she's the one who started keeping the list of who was born and who married who and so on, starting with what she believed to be her own birth date and the date she thought Alice and Linnie were born, and later she transferred the list to this bible. When she died in 1925, the bible came to my mother's sister, and from her to my mother. But we never knew anything about any diary. We knew Lucinda had taught herself to write obviously, but she was so oral; we thought the genealogy was the only thing she ever wrote. She never spoke about anything else... but look at what Dennis drew. Lord, they're almost exactly the same, and he didn't see what I was holding my finger over. Lester told me what the marks were underneath her initials, said she had placed the hieroglyphs in a—a what baby?"

"A cartouche honey."

"Right, a cartouche, this circle... Lester, you know the facts will always out. Our history may finally be telling itself through Dennis."

"Mama, is there any more spaghetti?"

"Zip, how can you think about food now honey?"

"Sounds like to me mama all three of yall planning a pretty long day for me. I need some fuel. Where's the hot sauce?"

Lester cleared his throat and spoke.

"Ah, look Dennis, I didn't mean to go off on you earlier, but um not used to people like you. You'd think I woulda handled the whole thing better cause I got a lotta practice in situations like this today. I been black all my life and Afro-American lives are so unreal that they're better than fiction. So what did you used to do in college?"

"Les, it's just a long story you don't wanna hear."

"No, no, really I do."

Through a spaghetti muffler, Zip tried to scream,

"Oh my god! Pop, don't ask him that ques—"

But is was too late. Dennis had already settled back in the dining room chair, fixed his intense blue eyes on Lester's dark brown ones, and opened his mouth.

Lester was doomed.

* * *

"... my parents... there's not time for all that Dennis. Don't you think that post-Lapsarian librarian is looking at those plans right now? Don't you know she's tryin to figure out why we want to see them so bad? Plus, my parents still think you're unbalanced anyway. They'd freak out if I took you home again. Whew! You're right though; we are foul. Whew! You know you're funky when you can smell yourself. But we don't smell any worse than anybody else in this place. Now about this treasure, let me tell you something— "

"— Hey man, I got some fire chickenhead here. Take a pop, won't cost you much."

"Naw, no thanks. Prechate it though."

"Zip, what the hell is 'chickenhead'?"

"Some powerful Columbian dope perked with that synthethic shit they use on the Space Shuttle platelets. Just keep smiling. Don't do nothin rude to these people. Now, like I was sayin— "

"— Ooo, salt and pepper. Don't yall wanna date? $100'll get you both in at the same time."

"Ah, no thanks. (Hey Zip, that is the ugliest whore I've ever seen.)"

"That's cause you're used to those HBO ho's. Ain't no pretty street prostitutes. Get it outta your head. Now, that treasure to you is one thing, but let me tell you what it is for me— "

"Excuse me gentlemens, yall— "

"Look, I don't know you. Don't say shit to me. Get outta my face. Fuck you!" screamed Zip.

("Zip, I thought you said be polite. Now look atcha.")

"Well damn main, you ain't got to talk to me like um no ho or nothin. A person can't speak to you or somethin? Just say 'I don't know you, I don't wanna talk to you.' You ain't got to cuss at me. I ain't no bitch. If you wanna fight or somethin, that's cool too!"

"Look, I didn't mean to offend you. Um just a little freaked ok? I just found out something bad— real bad. Let me show you this big sore on my dick— "

"Man, you keep yo dick in yo pocket! I don't wanna see nothin on yo dick. Let me get my ass outta here. These niggers in this bus station crazy!"

"Now, like I was sayin Dennis, we got to get that treasure no matter what it takes. We can't fuck it up. We got to be cool. You look around this terminal. This is what happens to poor people in America— especially black people. You've already lost me my job, and this is my one chance to hit it bigger and faster than I ever would have singin in clubs. Look around you. We mess this up, and *you* might be able to get a job somewhere makin 8 g's a year at some community college for a few years til they phase out your temporary position there and kick you out in the cold and in the same hour hire 20 others just like you. Me, I mess this up, and I'll be just another nigger down at the BlackDog bus station suckin dicks for a living."

"You're exaggerating."

"Of course I am. I'm trying to make a point."

* * *

Look, we gotta get downtown to Beale. I know I can get a gig at B.B. King's tonight and make a coupla hundred dollars. Come on let's go.

In that stinking thing that was once so called as Beale Street, a haven for the Cherokees' natural culture that led them to nothing but disaster, later a place for the Germans and Scotch that the Brits couldn't stand to look at, and then, a startling black epoch of black-seeming talent and businesses, really based in the in the hands of white-supremacists who still couldn't believe how blessed they had become through mainforce and Manifest Destiny, and finally into this THING that now shook and vibrated to a corporate cacophony as a thing unrhythmic, Beale Street was now underwritten by the very descendants, the sons and daughters, of the very people who had destroyed the tenor of Beale over and over whenever it became too black.

Ah , well, I know, I know, this is America and that is what we are about…
and yet some places still; when the roar from the monorail bearing the name
of a prominent local constabulary was not too rumbling, when the stink
that came from the river-washed intersection of Beale and Riverside did not
force you to turn walk back and north on Main, when the gang members
at Beale and Fourth were not killing tourists with the stray bullets meant
solely for each other, when he, himself, or she, herself, were not too far gone
on gin and supremacist-induced depression, still and still you might hear an
African moaning or strumming on hand-made instrument the essence of all
that that is all there is to life summed up in 12 bars.

Zip was rebuffed in his own home again for being too much of in the
present of what tourists and corporate types paid extreme sums for to hear
from the past. Too black, too R & B was old news for anyone of the post-Hip
Hop nation who had tried to bring contemporary black music to the street
that had given life to black music. Posing with women from the Coalition of
100 Black women at the photo shop of Club Willie Mitchell's was good for
$250 and drinks, and that would have to do.

So for tourists there could be no real R&B, just a facsimile of BLUES
that was both comforting and distancing, not too black, not too white, not
too modern, not too anything. The Blues had faded long ago into the CD
collections of suburban and foreign people who used it for whiskey-sipping
music and faded into the cultural crevices of a people on their way up whose
own children no longer understood the meanings of the words.

* * *

Siedah grabbed the edge of the Emory Special Collections desk. She
felt faint. Words were squeezed through her teeth like tempered daggers.

"What-do-you mean-the-Jones'-manuscript-is-no-longer-here?"

"Just what I said Miss. It's on loan. They took full liability coverage
out on the manuscript. And he's a well-known southern scholar. We didn't
mind."

"Who-are-THEY?!"

Chapter 10

"I want you to know this whole thing is strictly a loan— with interest." Unable to reply as he swallowed his cold chicken, unwilling to get in yet another argument about the NEED for the entire ordeal, Dennis stared out the tinted window as Turner Stadium faded from view and a giant Coke sign confirmed the edge of downtown Atlanta. A quick cab ride to Emory, a flash of his invalid _____ University ID with the valid dates "accidentally" faded, and then right back on the night express to Memphis, and, maybe, in a couple of months, with brains and luck, he could be in Rio, tanning and initiating himself in Vodoun, as his Swiss bank account number rested comfortably in the hotel safe. As far as Dennis was concerned, as soon as they found what they were looking for, Zip could go straight to hell business rate.

"And another thing, you meet me back here at the bus station in 3 hours. Is that enough time?"

"Yeah. Where are you going?"

"I gotta stop by Mr. Hugh's an see if I can patch things up a bit in case this thing is a rip. Then by the automatic teller again. You oughtta fall down on your knees every morning and thank god for automatic-tellers, else we wouldn't be here."

* * *

"Zip, Zip baby! How did everything go? What was the deal you were so close-mouthed about? Everybody's been comin in the past week askin about you. The rumor is you been in L.A. recordin an album. But I knew what was up. Well?"

"Look baby, we ran into a little bit of a logistics problem, but my partner is over at Emory straightening that out right now. And the next time you see me, I'll have two tickets in my pocket for L.A. for both of us. When the record starts climbin, we'll wait for Vegas to call. No road tours. I'm about traveled out for the duration. Ah, is your daddy, er, I mean, Mr. Hugh in?"

"Zip baby, Mr. Hugh's in, but Mr. Hugh said Mr. Hugh don't never wanna see you no more. Mr. Hugh said, 'That's just what Mr. Hugh gets for takin a mongrel dog in off the street. Mr. Hugh know he's gon throw up on the carpet the minute Mr. Hugh getsim inside cause he ain't use to nothin and don't know how to appreciate nothing.' That's what Mr. Hugh said and you know how Mr. Hugh is when Mr. Hugh verbalizes: if it's able to fight its way to Mr. Hugh's lips, Mr. Hugh means it. Oh, I don't know what to do."

"Well who's performing now? Who took my place? Mr. Hugh's gotta have somebody."

"Well, I mean, I've been carrying on by myself, and we have to get the police to scrape the men off the sidewalk 5 minutes after I come on every night. They like my voice and they like my legs— but it's all your doin Zip, you taught me stuff, brought me out. Got me off that stale-ass piano and put me on the Yamaha and the Moog. You made me get from behind the bar and look myself in the eye. Nobody ever believed in me enough to help me do that."

"Yeah, I can help everybody else find what they're lookin for, but I can't help myself. Look, I didn't do nothing but help speed up what was gon out in its own time anyway. You talented and you black: you cannot be denied."

Zip held her face in his hands and smiled. "You stealin from me girl? You doing **DONNEL**?"

"Every night in every show. And a lot of Regina Belle. And a whole lot of Debbie Gibson. The guys eat that stuff up. She's the biggest thing in the world again. Who woulda thunk it?"

"Well, um not gon confront your daddy in this condition— um poor and um funky. Lessee, get the key to the dressing room, and bring me a towel and some soup please mam. Umon change, make a stop, and then get back to the bus station. When I see Mr. Hugh, umon have a AMEX platinum hologram card and make him go to L.A. as our manager. That's just the kinda man I need on my side: A Don King clone."

* * *

"Zip, when you were gone, did you think about me?"

"(Glurb)… every second that I wasn't thinking bout myself… (Splatt)…"

"Well, whada you wanna do about us.?"

"(Spritt)… it's Spring outside and I think us is fine. Don't you think (Brrt) we better leave 'real good' alone (**HOOOEEEEEEBRRRTTT!**)?"

"Yea, I guess. Potential lovers and partners is better than divorced and pissed. You so gross. But you *do* keep a beat."

But then she started to think about it. You usually get so few chances in life to build up good sex stories for your grand-children, and here she was gonna let a prime character who could walk her around the room in his hands and carry whole scenes by himself slip out of the novel without giving them a chance to develop the plot-line.

Hanging out with him was ok. Playing and singing with him was fine. His conversation was better than TV. Looking at him in his jump-suit was great. But those were all "in lieu ofs." Substitutes. Appendages without a trunk. They had both backed off of it cause when things start out so intimate they have no where to go but down. At least, that's what all the dull people who didn't really enjoy making love in the first place said about love-making. If that lie were true, then the spiralling divorce rate was finally explained.

But she was the exact opposite of dull, always had been, and had never played the game this way before. What to do?

Peggy opened the shower door.
"Ah, Zip honey, here's your towel?"
"Where, I can't see nothin. I got soap in my eyes."
"Just reach your hand out… no honey, lower. Right. You feel it?"

"Ah. Peggy honey. Um not tryin to say um smarter than you or anything, but ah, I can tell you for a fact that that ain't no towel you just put my hand on."
"I asked you can you feel it."
Something different. Something to tell your grand-children about when they come to your house for Sunday dinner intimating that their generation had just invented sex.
So they worked and they sang while they worked. And the duet went like this:

"If one moment can be a lifetime
let my life be like this.
If all that I ever wanted could be mine
Let this moment be it…

You move like an angel
you kiss like the night

If one moment can be a lifetime
let this moment be so right

CHORUS:
Oh baby you feel so good, so half of me.
When you move, oh baby, you really move me.
I don't know what you doin, please just don't stop
I want what you givin, gonna give you all I got.
END CHORUS.

If one moment can be a lifetime,
and my life was to end right now,
I'd take this moment of a lifetime—no regrets,
No complaints. Just you and me—oh wow."

REPEAT CHORUS
REPEAT CHORUS
FADE

* * *

When Zip got back to the bus station, the first thing he saw was Dennis lying flat on the parking lot behind the tires of a cranking express to New Orleans. Was he hurt? Was he dead? Or was he just drunk?

"Dennis!" Pulling him out from under and setting him up, "Dennis, are you drunk? You trying to die? Huh, what? What are you saying? ENUNCIATE!"

"… just 'sound and— … busssh…— nyfing nothing'. Nuoleeens,— leens— uscript. Um just down here struttin and frettin… on loan… New Orleans…"

"Dennis what's wrong man? Ooowee you smell! That ain't liquor. What did you— oh no. Carbon monoxide! I gotta get you to the hospital.

"— no! Fuck the hospital… just… two tickets… New Orleans… two tickets… manuscript… express… on loan… (belch-fart)… "

* * *

And though others couldn't see it on this Georgian night as black as oil, intense anger manifested as nova-like heat lasered down from a DC-9 and met in mid-air frustration as spewing volcanic lava which erupted through the cab of a bus headed southwest on I-85.

Chapter 11

H igh, black, Anne Klein heels that would stand for no nonsense this morning impatiently stamped their barely visible pear imprints onto the tiled elevator floor.

In the stain-filled stair-well two concrete feet away from her, two Stacy Adams and two Adidas raced up six flights, the entire lexicon of U.S. profanities rapid-firing roughly six feet above them.

_____
"6"
_____

Elevator door opens.

Stair-well door is jerked open.

Black heels strike the carpet headed for the "Special Collections" sign.

Stacy Adams and Addidas pop onto carpet, see the sign.

Zip, looking straight ahead, starts to softly croon: *"I have no vision of love without you… /"*

Synchronically, the sound waves reach an ear pulled open with gold and diamond, the smell of Giorgio fills the foyer.

!!

* * *

"(Puff) I'm Dr. Dennis Johnston from _____ University," brandishing his ID, a quick flash, "I understand you have the Lucinda Burnett-Jones' manuscript here on loan from Emory. Is that right? (Puff)"

"Yeah, that's right. What about it.?"

("Great, male or female, they're all the same. There must be a Special Collections Peoploid factory somewhere.) I would like to see it please. You see, I was working with the manuscript last week, and evidently Emory shipped it out to you Friday afternoon, thinking perhaps that I had finished my work, but, you see, I had not, and, well, I've traveled all the way down here to finish my work. It's a very important book I'm writing on the, ah, er, Negro presence in America. It'll only take me a half-hour or so to get what I need."

"Well, Dr. Jerry Ward is the one who had that book sent down here and he's in onea them cells workin on it now. You and he can work out use of the manuscript if you give me that university ID, your driver's license, a major credit card— Visa or American Express only— and leave all food and ink-writing devices here at the desk with me. Obviously, there's no smoking allowed in any part of the Xavier library."

"Ah, I— I don't have a Visa or American Express. Will a Sears card do? How about a university bookstore discount card?"

"Just what I said. Are you tryin to give me a hard time?"

"No sir! But I don't— hol on. Hol on a minute."

* * *

As hard as people had tried by the end of the century, even with the aid of company-sponsored Emo-Control counseling, and that new drug, *EmoNoMore* (over-the-counter), people— especially black people— couldn't get their hearts, heads, and endorphin glands regimented along strictly corporate and logical lines. In broad daylight at the beginning of this hard-hearted century, people still expressed the second most irrational of human frailties: love-at-first-sight.

Both Zip and Siedah would have labeled it as animal attraction. The explosion in the foyer certainly wasn't anything less— wild animal, Sabre-Toothed-Tiger-Attraction— but these post-contemporary types weren't about to admit that the tiger carried on its shoulder a dove, and that the dove told the tiger when to strike.

"When you sing, my layers sweat right down my back."

"I… er… your perfume makes my toes curl up in my Stacy Adams."

And with those etchable words for the spiralling stone tower of love-through-the-ages, they both fell on the carpet in full faint, two well-proportioned bundles of light-blue silk.

* * *

"Zip Zip, what's wrong with you? Wake up. Get offa that woman. Wake up!"

"Huh? What? I… whatchu want?"

"Gimme a credit card— Visa or American Express only."

"In my back pocket… where is she?"

"Up under you."

Dennis grabbed Zip's wallet and ran for the desk. Opening the wallet, he realized he'd never seen so many credit cards in his life. Broke as he was, he both pitied and envied those of extended, open-end credit.

"Are you Zip Peters?"

"No. He's over there on the floor."

"Well, he's gotta come over here and sign this voucher before you can go in. 'Zip.' What the hell kinda name is that?"

"Zip! Get up! Come over here! I need you!"

"Are you all right Miss?"

"Whew, I've never been better."

"Sorry about faintin on topa you. Don't know what came over me."

"Sorry about faintin under you. I know what came over me."

Helping her to her feet, he saw that when looking straight ahead, his eyes came even with the flesh just under her eyes. Even better. He loved a challenge. A mountain climber from way back, two thoughts came immediately to his mind as his eyes ascended to her layered peak, and down again, over the highlands, to her black, velvet heels. At this point, gosh, you can't rush into things, so he was only willing to admit one of the thoughts to himself: that this was not only the most beautiful woman he'd ever fainted on, but also this was the one for him. He could find stuff with this woman. The second point he pretended to ignore, skeptic that he was, and saved that epiphany for later. And a change over-took him and slammed him, but this change was unknown by him, who, even as he was sliding further down into the crystal hazel of Siedah's eyes, had forgotten his own name, and who was as oblivious to the other happenings in this Delta library reserve room as a the new butterfly is to its former ugly and tubular shape.

She, more honest and experientially-comfortable with affairs, held his hand like a vise. How ironic, how human, how positively... Negroid, she thought, to come back home and find that what you left looking for was right down the street all the time. How antithetical to post-WW II economic and intellectual expansion was the idea of staying within a 20 mile radius of your hometown and finding a good job *and* a good lover. Look at the man: curly black hair moving down that Gabonese/Italic-shaped head, past the chocolate eyes, to end in a perfectly-etched Teddy Pendergrass beard. The shoulders, the chest, the stuff, the legs, the posture. And all with that voice! "Sorry I fainted on you" he says, and your nipples burst through your Tahari blouse. In her head, Moogs were backing up Stevie Wonder as he sang "Overjoyed;" Debby Allen jumped over her head and dropped rose petals; Robin Leach showed them available palaces in the Caribbean. Yes, yes, now here was a man she could love.

"Look, I gotta run over here for a second and sign something. You not gon go away are you?"

"I'm going to Special Collections, too. I'll walk with you."

"Dennis, what the hell's the problem? I got other things on my mind right now."

"Just sign this Visa imprint and I'll be back in a minute."

While Zip signed, Siedah spoke:

"Ah, sir, I need to see the Lucinda Jones manuscript for a whole 10 minutes." And then she, nodding to Zip, "Now, don't you go anywhere Zip. This is only gonna take a minute."

Zip and Dennis were *LIFE* magazine stills.

"Well, mam, you're gonna have to wait in line behind these two, ah, gentlemen. They're waiting to see that manuscript now."

*"WHAT DO **YOU** WANT WITH THAT MANUSCRIPT!!!"* Zip, Dennis, and Siedah screamed in triplicate.

"Shhh, keep your voices down or I'll call security. Honestly, 'scholars!' Never met a one ofem who had decent personal hygiene."

"Why do yall want to see the manuscript? Are you two engineers?" asked Siedah. "Are you from ANGCO? Huh? You tryin to move in on this bid? I shoulda known it was all too good to be true. And me getting paid double for this job! This whole two weeks has been nothing but one big pain in my fine ass after another, and now it's tryin to go for my heart."

"We're not engineers," Dennis sputtered, "we're scholars working on a book to which this manuscript is vital. It's about the, ah, calligraphy of antebellum black women. Are you trying to horn in on our research. I've had one book stolen from me already. Did _____ University send you?"

"Piss off dandruff head. I'm an engineer, and all I wanna do is check the stress points in the roof design of the house of this dead woman's rebel ancestor, and then I think um gonna change careers to something less stressful, like maybe air-traffic control or alligator wrestling."

"— didn't mean to shout at you Siedah. It's just, we've been traveling all over the world trying to find this old book and— "

"— Tell ME about traveling."

"— and, well, we're a little tired; you can look at the thing first if you're in a hurry."

"Zip are you crazy? You don't even know this woman."

"I know all I need to know about this woman. I believe her."

"What do yall care? Um not gonna eat the book. After I'm through with it, yall can read it for a million years for all I care. What's so important about this book?"

"It's … ah … look, if you really wanna know, can Dennis go in there and examine the book while I tell you all about it?"

"Well … I guess you can talk to me any time baby."

"Zip are you crazy? What did you pop last night on the bus? (Now you look asshole, half of this endeavor is mine. Anything she extorts outta you comes outta your half. Uh, uh, uh, um glad I didn't faint on her first, or it'd be comin outta my half. Look at that woman.)"

("You don't know nothing. Why, you can look at this fox and tell she's a Sunday school girl. She ain't evil. I believe every word.")

"Yeah, right." Dennis rolled his eyes, and then his mind took him back to the … IT.

Siedah turned to Dennis.

"Look, Dennis?, is that your name, well Dennis honey, you go on in— but don't take all day— and I'll stay out here and see what Zip has to say."

The librarian blurted in.

"He can't use it all day. It's on hold for Dr. Ward in the mornings and others can only see it for an hour at a time in the afternoons. It'll be a miracle if Dr. Ward lets him see it now for a second. Man holds and rubs that book like it's a mojo or something."

Zip shot out words in a whisper from the side of his mouth toward Dennis.

("Dennis, when you get the photos, umon spank this librarian's ass with onea Amy Vanderbilt's thick books.") And then from the other side of his mouth:

"Thank you sir. But Dr. Johnston is very persuasive, and I'm sure Dr. Ward is a very understanding man cause he's interested in Afro-American literature."

"Hey you, your limit's not up on this Visa is it?" the librarian whined at Zip as Dennis rushed past the desk. "If he damages anything in that manuscript, it's got to go on this card's account."

"No sir. It's clear. It's got a 5 thousand dollar limit. I don't charge anything on it. I just pay the annual fee to build up my credit rating."

"Zip honey, come over here and sit in the lounge with me. I wanna hear all about you— I mean about the manuscript."

"Well... ," walking into the smoke-filled, junk-food haven, where anemic-looking, unemployed people with glasses on stared out the window and wondered why they ever bothered to learn how to read, "... um gon have to take you back to my childhood in a way. You see, we weren't very rich. In fact..."

* * *

21

And so as I close, I hope that some of our POWERFUL, white breth'ren can see the injustices done to our family line. Our LORD and SAVIOR, JESUS CHRIST, spake no truer nor sterner words than when HE saith: "As ye do unto the least of these, so also ye do unto ME.' And who among you, aye though you be the finest and richest, wish to bring the Wrath of the ALMIGHTY down on your feeble heads?

Not retribution, but rightful remuneration for all pilfered Capital and Properties is what I ask in the name of Right and Justice. A murderer, slaver, coward, and liar built up a vast fortune through my swarthy kindred in general, and through his own dark KITH and KIN in particular. I ask only what is rightfully mine through fairness and lineage.

If any of my white breth'ren, long succored by me and mine, be moved by my sad and doleful tale to do what all the world knows is CHRISTIAN, I do, here, by this Heaven-inspir'd writ absolve them, their ancestors and descendants, of all previous transgressions that may be legally binding, and do sincerely wish the Lord's blessing on each and every one of them.

— finished this day by my own hand,
September 13, 1922.
Lucinda Burnette-Jones, Widow, Oakland

"Truly amazing."

Tears ran down the face of the ancient black scholar, and he was quick to absorb them with his linen handkerchief with the initials **JWW** before they stained a text that already contained enough sadness for a thousand people for a thousand years.

He was always moved to tears when he read any non-fiction by blacks. And the stuff just never got any lighter. North or South, pre-war, post-war, late 19th-century, early 20th, even into the warp-speed 21st-century, male or female, there were the same complaints, the same atrocities, the same… dignity. And they argued not only for fairness and a less-stressful life for themselves, but for the very people who were beating, raping, cheating and robbing them. Truly amazing. Nothing seemed to change in fact for blacks as it changed in the fiction that others called their history books. As soon as one illegal door was closed, two more legal doors through which blacks could be kicked in the ass were opened.

"… and her letters to her friends and known family appended at the back… they… the perception she had… and the way she expressed the pathos of a human being made into a thing… blacks make the strangest slaves and oppressed class whites have ever known. Just plain unchangeable, yet changing all the time, clinging to life over impossible odds, as though they still remembered across the millennia the stoicism taught in the schools of Abydos, and the sacred spells of countenance recited in the Temples of Memphis. Truly amazing. I guess there's nothing you can do with people who dance in the face of bullets… either killem all to the last child or lovem… — huh? Yes, come in please."

"Ah, excuse me. Dr. Jerry Ward?"

"Yes."

"I'm Den— er, Dr. Dennis Johnston from _____ U. May I interrupt your study for just a moment please suh?"

* * *

"… and they must have not realized that I wasn't quite finished… and, well, if I could just finish examining the manuscript at your convenience… I…"

"Sure, sure son. It's time for me to go to lunch anyway. Here, knock yourself out. Ha, I'll try to get Sam to give you more than an hour. What did you say your work is concerned with again?"

"Ah ... the comparative prose structures of 19th- and early 20th-century Afro-American writers."

"Sounds like real bullshit to me. At your age you just finishin your dissertation?"

"Oh no sir... I... just think it's important work."

"Yeah, well, God bless you. Just be careful you don't starve. I made my career on literary theory myself. But the '70s were different times. I used to hesitate to do Afro research, real hard to get a job doin that kinda thing at one time. You won't believe me, but the powers-that-were would punish you professionally, run your work into the ground, say it lacked relevance. At the same time they'd try to push you into only that one area of teaching and research cause they didn't want your black ass breathing down their specialty areas, and since you were black they asserted that that's all you could teach—how to be black in Afro-American literature courses—knowing all the time that in fact Afro literature instruction was much more rigid than other areas cause it was a new area just being codified and was as "valid" as any other literature; plus you had zero chance of being tenured or promoted if you taught only Afro-American literature. It was all so frustrating and complicated... and I was once a coward about so many things...

Now, unless they can make me a light-skinned Negro in an all-black neighborhood on his bike a long way from home at 8 p.m. on April 4th 1968 in Memphis, I don't figure they understand punishment. Shit, I already been to hell and lived to tell. I don't wanna go to the mortician til I finish this work on the narrational link between the slave narratives and the Harlem Renaissance. Just to do homage to my dead parents and remind myself that um an Afro before I kick off. One more thing son."

"Yes sir?"

"I hope you got a handkerchief."

Chapter 12

While Dennis pestered the people at Fast-Lab to hurry up and get the negatives developed and enlarged, Zip marveled at the techno-trappings of Siedah's N.O. condo. Everywhere books and CDs and sculpture and paintings. Furniture post-contemporary. No nod to what wasn't happening, that is, the past. Unless you considered all the Kushite-motif underpinnings, which were so ancient and rare that they looked as though they had come from the future. (What was that Picasso had said about all his cubist stuff being African art?) And 200 pair of Evan Picone high-heels everywhere in every color.

Who was this person, Siedah, and why was she provoking this straining inside Zip's chest and why was she making him daydream?

* * *

"Tonight as I sit here with the sweet smell of you on my hands and mustache I move toward what I want to become… so that I can be ready to be allowed to be all that I already am.

Was there a time before when things weren't so confused, so unstuck? If were're smarter now than we've ever been, why can't we think our way out of situations that we never asked to be in in the first place, never coulda dreamed until they so awfully were?

When you were my fellow thief and you helped me steal those immutable moments with you those nights on your desk in the office where you worked, I almost knew… I almost knew. My truest self is freed when I am most who and what and where I need to be, but oh those stolen seconds so unconnected, so interrupted, baby, so far apart.

If you had asked me to dream what I live, I woulda woke up screaming 'It's only a nightmare, only day-time shades out to spook me, who go away when I open my eyes!'

But I open my eyes and my nightmare is wide awake, screaming down the avenue with the hammer down, and all I can think to do is get out of the way.

But if you ask me to take one of our seconds and see it secretly for all its sides, then I know. I know. I know. And I move without moving like an angel on helium.

When I first realized who and what I was to be I was 3 and my father was snapping a picture of me; a little black metal Kodak it was cause they couldn't throw anything away, and he froze me for all time in that little black box that later produced a hard copy of me and my mother holding this boy who didn't need to see the b/w photo to know that this was summer and the Johnson grass was green and Bobwhites hollered and the sounds of the last of the cotton buses gave audio to an emotional moment that didn't need sound because that moment sang from a piece of 1-dimensional Kodak paper because it was perfect and alive; a boy who didn't need to be told in the KJV Biblical analogues in which his parents always spoke that winter would come because he already knew that at the height of summer when it was prettiest and greenest, it was then that the Johnson grass would cut you to pieces, and that every sunflower you wanted to sniff might hold a bee."

So this boy 3, who could see, froze that ***emotional moment*** and went back to pick it up in a world where he needed such moments constantly. But frozen emotional moments are safe only so long as you don't expand, don't grow. And everybody who was gonna be anybody had to grow. While his playmates grew vertically and 1-dimensionally, he grew horizontally, porously, and multi-dimensionally, absorbing every emotional moment like a sponge, synthesizing every micro-emo to evolve and conjure himself into what he had to become to face winter.

And when hair started to grow on his face, he realized that his time was filled with exotic moments that left him wondering and wide awake. ***Exotic Moments*** come to us because they must as we expand into a sphere where there is no room for difference and only minute time to live and die. As we sprout our first facial hairs and little tiny breasts, moments become exotic because they are so far removed from the way we perceived the world to be; and we must push our perceptions through the tiny interstices of the FOR-REAL, almost solid world.

And he knew what any honest contractor will tell you: that in the hardest, best-laid concrete there are holes that water and worms will find and go through to reach their most desired states. The worms would *eat* the concrete if they had to. And this boy, having been a worm in the enemy's concrete since he saw the light, knew that with genius and luck, his water would reach its own levels, and then he could burp out the excess concrete.

The biggest exotic moment was growing to accept that concrete was destructible. Once you accepted this, you expanded and nothing could stop you.

The second biggest exotic epiphany happened when you had to face the fact that the world was concrete squares, and you had to work to be inventive enough to be allowed to be a circle, or a triangle, or whatever the hell it was that you most naturally were cause them squares intended to make you just like them, or crush you into dust, and then go back to their gin and 3rd daily broadcast of *Tyra*.

But, hell, without contraries there's no progression, so you figured out typically-Afro ways to sidestep, circumvent, and generally transform these exotic moments. The squares didn't destroy you and the moments were exotic because all that came after the explosion of the squares' awfulness meeting your side-stepping was beautiful and never-before-known. And it was all yours, and to be exotic again the world would have to come up with something you hadn't figured out how to sidestep.

And then you laughed your ass off in the jacuzzi at the old-folks home over a passed life honestly-spent and tried to explain to your immensely dense, over-educated grandchildren that they had to live life as a private *secret* or they'd be stuck in a public death for 3 score and 10.

"But way before the triumph of the country club jacuzzi, when I learned that **emotional moments** were far too brief and seductive and limited mainly to memory, and that *exotic moments* would thrill me and haunt me for all of the adult phase, I knew I had to find something… something that would allow me to be me. And then I was sorry for laughing at all the suckers all my life who kept stumbling around talking about they were 'looking for something.' I'd always thought myself better and stronger, and yet there I was, a perfect candidate for the "Advisor" section in *Ebony*.

And then it came to me when I was 16 and I knew, I knew, I knew. And I was made whole and ready for the world as it was. **EROTIC MOMENTS** came to me, took me, blew me away forever.

Erotic moments come to me like the pure and infallible voice of a whippoorwill reminding me that it's the proof of things wished for that makes me cling to the hopeful part of life, that the erotic is the real thing: the most beautiful and truest poet can be one who only sings in natural chords and who never writes a word. And if I hear it once I thrill to it forever.

Erotic moments come to me, a long banquet table at the Bon Chateau in New Orleans, down St. Charles and tucked in a dark alley where only people of like-minds know to go. Stiff white table cloth and rows and rows of wonder in front of my eyes. And if I eat it once I savor it forever.

Everything in front of me is legal, but we all scoot our chairs for the shadows and nobody talks, nobody asks questions. In front of us, courses and courses of delight: Gulf shrimp smothered in sweet sauce and Galliano, Oysters Bienville, paired squares of river cat soaked in brandy, alligator soup thick with large chunks of white potatoes and tail, frog legs stuck in pineapple, cornish hens soaked for 3 days in lemon sauce, baked medium and stuffed with sweetbread and lemon pulp, a long broiled grouper split and stuffed with corn muffin sprinklings soaked in real butter, big silver containers of warmed soy and orange sauce in easy reach, long rolls of chocolate jelly-cake with black icing and coconut sprinkles around every inch of cake, a whole cheese cake cooked thick with all its texture and sweetness compressed into only a 3 inch height with a quarter-inch thick vanilla wafer crust and crystal goblets of homemade ice cream on the side; then French coffee so thick and black served in rectangular china cups with a representation of the smiling, sword-in-hand Maid of Orleans hand-painted on the side of each.

Erotic moments come to me, FloJo rockets one-legged like a laser in races where she is only competing with herself, at speeds where her blur metamorphoses and turns into Michael Jordan who with a move as sweet and smooth as satin goes through, up, and over the Celtics to leave their green mouths hanging in awe and shake the world with a dunk set-up by the devil's pick, and then to see him land before the ball touches the court, like a giant brown feather he lands and then moonwalks backwards up the court.

Erotic moments come to me and they make life last forever. Sensually taking you and me with all our clothes on but no underwear down to your leather-topped desk in slinky sweat and fragranced memory—no in-lieu-ofs, no insteads—but every substitute we provide each other almost as good as our usual goodness, every new thing some unknown sweet secret revealed only inside you and me,   and eroticmomentscomeandIhavesuchagoodmemoryandIhaveamillion moments,

they take us down and
eroticmomentscome,
but, Tall and Fine, I'll let you write this one for us.
And if I feel it once I come forever.

* * *

What makes people want to try to make a go of love these days when the realities of the world destroy illusions of stability and positive self deceit— two of the three tripod legs that keep love new and shiny through the bad breath in the morning and the gray reports of "only 17" blacks killed by other blacks in the preceding Central African night—and deny any logic in attempting to do anything warm and honorable?

Zip knew the inherent dangers of defeat and letdown involved in actually trying to "LOVE" someone, but as he fingered the lines of the Romare Bearden color print, he felt himself falling, falling, falling. Taking chances was nothing new to him [Wasn't that how he'd ended up in this crazy triangle in the first place?], but he wanted to know what it was about *this* 20-minute-workout-girl-with the briefcase full of super-structure plans and mathematical print outs he wanted to know what it was about *her* that was unsettling enough to make him want to take a chance on something, that, if it worked out, kept you smiling til you died, and, if it messed up— which it had a 99% chance of doing—kept you in the child support court, the nose candy, and drunkenly reading bad, bad, confessional poetry from the '60s until you dropped dead from sheer depression.

* * *

"They say to know a woman, you should check out the men she hangs around with. You got anything you want to tell me? I mean, you know, before I start askin you how you want your eggs in the mornin?"

"Nothing about that you don't already know and that you know you don't want me to repeat. I'm a syncretic Afro with spiritual ties to Kenya and Frank Sinatra records. Nobody comes here without calling first, and both those toothbrushes in the bathroom are mine. I love to play, but if we're gonna play, you gotta wear your raincoat in the storm. What about yourself; do I need to add more deadbolts to the condo door?"

"Nah, I always been too mature to make people expect more than I could give. I've always been roped in by the reality that you ought to be rich before you start talking about staying with one person, cause Ziplings can't be far behind. At least if you're rich you don't have to see your own black children on TV hugging Sally Struthers and begging for jobs."

"You trying to tell me you a virgin?"

"Naw, I got at least 200,000 miles on me, but I've got plenty of oil and um well lubed. Don't have no dents cause I give my lovers exactly back what I take. Keep us both honest and workin good."

"Shoot, I was kinna hoping for something new."

Siedah laughed and deftly dropped her satin without taking her eyes from his eyes. Without looking, she leaned back against the edge of her high-tech, solid mahogany desk, and propped herself up on its edge using only her shoulder muscles. Her high-heeled feet opened first a lower drawer to her right and then an upper drawer to her left. She put her right foot on the edge of the lower drawer. Then she put her left foot up high on the upper left drawer, and dangled a light-blue high-heel off her left toes as her right foot came to rest on the lower drawer.

Zip knew that if that shoe dropped it was his ass.

"Baby, um brand new," Zip murmured, his reason for living now finally opening up before him.

"Then prove yourself to me," Siedah growled.

Zzzip.

* * *

: *sweat, shoulders, knees, toes, eyebrows, lips, navels, sides, mouths, eyes, hair, tongues, fuzz, spit, backs, hands, noses, nails, butts, 16 fingers, ears, muscles, eyelids, flesh, stomachs, thighs, collar bones, heads, ankles, necks, teeth, skin, calves, lashes, 4 thumbs, points and conclaves.*

: *mirrors, Antaeus, angles, bracelets, headboards, pillows, untucked sheets, carpet, knocked-down pictures, sinks, rooms, doorknobs, shower curtains, linoleum, baby oil, K-Y Jelly, "Love Zone" by Billy Ocean, entertainment centers, candles, honey, Giorgio, ice cubes, 3 burning logs, purple garters, cocoa butter, black bikini briefs, "You Bring Me Joy" by Anita Baker, crumpled drapes, desks, scissors, body paint, a razor, "ENTRY May 4" in This Is My Beloved by Walter Benton, window sills, bathtubs, shaving cream, sheet burns, Emanuelle In Bangkok (Uncut European version), stuffed animals, dressers, Queen Anne chairs, white stockings, "Anyone Who Had A Heart" as sung by DONNEL, real cold Roederer Estate, and a jar of peanut butter.*

: *a reaffirmation of the innate and absurd yet vitally necessary notion that the world is an* **OK** *place to live, the willingness to disbelieve all the badness your intelligence and experience have already confirmed are true, "Uh, uh, uh, will you look at that," time slows down, an atomic bomb blast couldn't move the two of you from underneath the quilt by the fireplace, views of the human body that you ain't supposed to see, "I didn't know the loving was gonna be this long," the Spring-time view at dusk from Denzel Washington's Central Park West condo, Chinese food at midnight with* The Wolfman *in the DVD, "Whatever it is you want me to do, just tell me," the inability to stop telling about your past and the inability to stop telling the truth, the feeling of not being alone, a $4500 sound system (21st-century yuan) in the back seat of a chauffeur-driven 860 Mercedes at midnight on the Golden Gate Bridge, Kenya in April, your mother's ham (with pineapples and yams) on Christmas, May rain dripping from the house into a puddle by your open bedroom window, "Ooo, that's a good-looking guy," Aretha singing "Call Me" on a portable CD as you're jogging around Cape Cod, the moon rising over beachfront Miami as seen from the* QE II, *"This is my favorite," Rio at Carnival. And a partridge in a pear tree.*

: broken type-writer keys, liquid paper stains, just *the edge of the tip of a ball-point, bent lamps, mailing labels stuck on your ass, new uses for the round hole in the ruler and the large pieces of art gum, the complete and total bio/ techno merging of computer technology and the most ancient horizontal dance of Isis (Aset) and Osiris (Asar) that fertilized the entire Nile Delta, bruised knees, paperclip imprints, sweat, new positions, the willingness to take a chance on being completely embarrassed in front of your friends, and the wisdom to remake the world.*

* * *

A 30 minute wait:
Rewind. More of the same—only better.

* * *

"Whew its hot and funky in HERE! Why don't chall turn the air on?" Dennis moved toward the window in Siedah's living room that faced green and lush St. Charles Avenue, laughing low and shaking his head.

"It is on. It's just a little humid in here," Siedah said, as she lay stretched back in the brass dining room chair staring at Zip's chest, legs and bulge; Zip opposite her, equally stretched, alternately staring at her breasts—close-cropped and bulging beneath her purple Spandex—and at the *Dark Side of the Moon* prism picture she'd had handcopied onto the dining room ceiling. Their bodies were there with Dennis, but their minds were still back in sweatland.

Dennis leaned back on the windowsill and spoke.

"Ok, we've got a copy here of the whole 89 pages: she talks about her only son, and we can easily trace him to your mother Zip, cause that was her 1st cousin—er, and great uncle or something—born in Fayette County, so we can get those records a few minutes away from Memphis, plopem in front of the Matron with this copy, and we're on our way. Zip, are you listening?

"She talks about the design of the Winchester house here, but I don't know if what she says is gonna help us. Let's see here ... her cousins and uncles workin all day and all night ... marble from Greece ... 2000 pounds of African Brass, not used ... half Roman parthenon, half French opera-house motif ... only 6 favorite slaves allowed in house after walls up and roof on ... 8 main roof beams ... 7 at 33 1/3 degree angles, one at 90° ... Uncle Menes puts his loa into roof beams ... Well what the hell does that mean?"

"It means, Dennis, whoever the slave Uncle Menes was he put his spiritual essence into the work he did. He put his whole self into something so that the something became a part of him; y'know, animism, transference, transfiguration, even transmigration. Them slaves was heavy boy." Zip struggled to bring himself back to the mundane problem of striving for wealth. First Siedah, now Menes; a busy day even for the ZipMan.

"Anyway, my mother would say that it kept those people a part of life, long after their bodies disappeared from this plane. She'd say it kept them from being enemies of nature, and, relatedly, enemies of other human beings, because they became one with nature and natural forces. She'd say that that house was more Menes's than Winchester's, and that, thus, the U.S. is more the Indians' than the Africans', and more the Africans' than the Anglos'. Whew! I've just had an into-outta-extra-body experience, so stop me if I start to sound like a Sunday night *National Geographic Special.*"

"Shit. That is heavy. What do you say Siedah?"

"I say, after tonight, I believe all things are possible." Siedah spoke with her eyes closed, holding her long fingers entirely closed around Zip's left ankle.

"And I say that there's a reason the details of that house, the concrete as well as the spiritual details, were purposely passed on through the generations to reach Lucinda. I say that there's more to those details than just a recitation of facts or legal proof that Lucinda's ancestors were the original builders—even if she didn't know she was telling us more than she knew. I say we need to brainstorm everything she mentions about the house and see if we can read in any clues." Siedah finished speaking and pulled herself up to the table and stared at Dennis. But what she was really thinking about was breakfast.

It didn't matter what time of day you had breakfast—it could be midnight—but you just had to have breakfast with your lover after the first time. Your first breakfast after the first time you've made love to somebody new is always the best breakfast in the world. It's The First Breakfast, you know, and you're like Aset and Asar and the whole garden is ripe and fresh and sweet. And it doesn't matter what time of day you eat this breakfast— well, you know damn well it's not gon be at the regular time cause your morning in that bed is filled with **NEWNESS** and you're gonna hold onto this **NEWNESS**—this thing that is so right and can't go wrong cause it's **NEW**—you're gonna hold onto this thing as long as you can and bear-hug every sweat drop out of it until it runs down his legs and you have to lick it off; like pineapple it tastes, a million clumps of cholesterol to clog your heart, but you don't care, and you lick and lick and lick til it's all gone.

Zip turned his head to the left to look at one of the primary reasons that life is good no matter how bad it is.

"Well, why don't we do that on the trip back to Memphis? You comin on the bus with us Siedah?" Dennis asked.

"The bus? You must have Alzheimer`s. In my clothes? I wouldn't survive 5 minutes. But I can't be separated from Zip right now, so we're all going to fly back together. I'll front you welfare waifs the airfare until you're rich. Oh, there'll be a reasonable rate of interest for both you and Zip of course."

Zip put on his best naive-boy-overpowered-by-the-older-experienced-woman face and voice: "But, but, we hardly know each other and you'd charge me interest? What kind of interest? What did you have in mind? We gotta go to church together a few times, let you meet the folks, see if my friends can get along with your friends. I HAVE GOT TO GET TO KNOW YOU BETTER."

"Isn't my wanting and loving you enough?" Siedah purred, lovely, serious.

Silence and smiles all around.

* * *

Dennis was jostled awake as the plane hit an air-pocket on its descent into Memphis International Airport. When he'd faded off 50 minutes before in this one hour flight, Zip and Siedah had excused themselves to go to the bathroom. As Dennis now nodded back out, his triad row of sets still had only himself as a member.

"Guess it was the gumbo …" Dennis mumbled as his head dropped onto his chest again and a child in the back of the plane whined to its father.

"But it's been **"OCCUPIED"** the whole flight! I gotta go pee daddy!"

And from behind the door a complaint:

"No Zip, you take that shirt off right now. You're cheating me out of my view."

* * *

Finally in the Memphis Room vaults, Zip and Siedah stared at the old plans of an antebellum mansion long ago burned to ashes. Only two could be in a cell at a time, and Dennis went about his assignment in the regular library, locating an expendable copy of a present day map of Memphis. Zip was to locate an 1860 map of Memphis while he was in the archives. Siedah wrote quickly, noting the stress points in the beams while Zip photographed the plans and then folded his arms in silence, pondering how the answer was encoded on this old piece of velum.

"Do you see anything that strikes you as odd about this design Siedah?"

"Well, it's an African-American hybrid; which is like saying its a glass window. I already explained to you about that on the plane."

"Right, but I guess I mean anything written or drawn on here that has nothing to do with typical engineering of the time, something that has nothing to do with building a house; in fact, something contrary to the construction or safety of a house."

"Well, I don't … I mean. Stuff looks pretty typical for area designs of that time. Rooms, doors, and windows, enormously large, as though they were building for giants. Just inventing the myth of themselves I guess. Granite columns way too strong and thick for the necessary front and back frame supports. Porches large enough to set eight slave cabins on them. Fireplaces big enough in every room for a blacksmith's shop. I just don't see anything particularly odd for an eclectic, rich slaver, except the beams, and we know the Africans did that on purpose."

Zip continued to stare at the plans. The veins in his head pulsated with energy that could not find a suitable verbal outlet.

"Look Zip, I don't see shit here. I've got what I needed and I'm gonna fax it to N.O. and take a week off: I'll hang out with you and Dennis. Maybe you'll find ... something. I already found all I want for the moment. God what a relief! Now, with the stress points located that restauranteur can have us design a new blueprint and get some contractor to rebuild this awful thing. I was about to go cra—"

Zip knew immediately that she knew, but he didn't know what she knew.

"Well, what! What! What! What is it? You see something?" he screamed.

"Zip, you've got the Jones' copy with you, right? Read me the part again that Dennis read about the layout of the house and Uncle Menes."

"... eight main roof beams, 7 at 33 1/3 degree angles and 1 at a 90° incline slanting down toward the front veranda"

"Wait. Stop right there!"

"It's obviously odd, but we went over that on the plane and didn't come up with anything. You say it was all part of the blackenization and that it didn't substantially weaken or strengthen the structure of the roof in any way."

"Yeah, I know; but it's so goddamed odd there's gotta be something there. Let's play with those figures for a minute 8, 7,1, 33 1/3, 90."

"The total is 139 1/3 Siedah."

"No kidding. What do you want? A cookie?"

"Well it's a start."

"Zip, that was the first thing I did in my head, and it didn't get me anywhere. Get you anywhere."

"No."

"Then come up with something else. It's in these figures I know it."

"Yassuh boss. Here's something for your ass: how about playing with the notion of the angles. Lessee, 33 1/3 degrees and 90 degrees? Anything?"

"Nothing but a headache. I'll bet old Winchester used to get a headache walkin through that house. The whole arch system of the house would make the average person dizzy, and that plunge at the front of the house; it musta seemed like you were falling over the edge ... of ... the ... world."

"Something?"

"The world ... this guy was building his own little 'Plantation Land' in DisneyWorld. I wonder if that ... Zip, quick, is there a map of the world in here or a globe? Something like that."

"Here's a globe right here."

Siedah's manicured, inchlong purple fingernails scratched through the polar ice until they came to a certain longitude line; then her right purple forefinger scratched the paper off Greenland, Canada, and Lake Superior. It stopped in Dixie. The forefinger of her left hand was simultaneously scratching through the mountains of China, scraping Lotus flowers from the bottom of the valleys in Japan, and then parting the Pacific, through luscious L.A., decimating lower Ruralia (all that topographical and intellectual emptiness west of the River), only to chip the paint on her right forefinger at a black dot as far southwest in Tennessee as you can go without falling into the tropical state The River is named after.

"Hamercy!" For the minute, Zip was ecstatic and his excitement confined to regional exclamations of joyous surprise long buried from his southern childhood. Then, as quickly as it came, the joy turned to frustration.

"Siedah, we already know the house was in Memphis. We got a pretty good idea too that the treasure is wherever the house was. Ha! This doesn't get us anywhere. All you've done is ruin a globe with those—ooo—fingernails of yours. What an anal retentive he must have been! What a wonderful secret! 'Figure out this clue and find that my treasure is in Memphis.' God, what a moron."

"No wait. Don't give up. **DON'T EVER GIVE UP!** Gimme that calculator outta my purse. I wanna know to the goddamed second where these longitude and latitude lines cross through Memphis. Waitaminit. Waitaminit. Zip, you got a local street map?"

"That's Dennis' job."

"Well, I'll go out and talk to him. I think I got it."

As Siedah reentered with the map, Zip blew a kiss at her, which she totally ignored, making Zip feel less guilty about trying to get up under her blouse while she frantically tried to match-up coordinates.

"IloveyouIloveyouIloveyou Siedah. I said that didn't I? I actually said that to somebody."

"Zippy, please not now silly. Oh shit, look at this. 5 minutes east, and 10.5 minutes south. That's where that line intersects, and on this local map its … right … here. Where's that?"

"Intersection of Haynes and Park. Sure I know where that is, but there's nothing there but a hardware store and a coin-operated car wash. I mean"

"That's right Zip baby.That's all that's there *now*. Baby I do believe we found it. Let's get Dennis and get outta here. I love you too baby. Ooo, it tastes just like honey when it rolls off your lips! Let's go! Let's go!"

* * *

"and another thing bitch, if you ever put your finger in my face again … a lotta good you're doing advancing the state of Western knowledge with your fat ass, harassing everybody who tries to go into the damned Memphis Room."

Siedah grabbed Dennis' arms and pulled him away from his diatribe.

"Dennis we ain't got time for that shit now. We know where it is— I mean, was. Come on."

"You know? You really know? Oh, um gonna buy only hardcover editions on acid-free paper from now on. Look out Rio!"

Zip pushed both of them through the door and ran them toward the rented 800 ZXX+.

"And don't worry about her," said Zip. She's going to get her due when she goes to reshelve that folio of old plans."

"What's 'her due?'"

"A big ball of snot on the cover for her eyes only."

"Ooo Zip you foul!" Dennis and Siedah howled.

* * *

"Yeah, but big money excuses all transgressions."

Chapter 13

On the soil of the Two-Lands, now *finally* again one land, 3000 years of Dynastic success stretched as far as any African eye wanted to see.

In the year 659 B.C., Khmt was the center of downtown San Francisco on New Year's Eve. It was the center of the center. If Khmtic citizens could dream it, they could have it, buy it, conquer it, or invent it. Khmt was the universe in 386,659 sq. miles. The only Khmtics to leave Khmt were those who were so thoroughly bored with the Dynastic Sameness of Success and the Infinite Path of Existence that they thought they should share some of that glory with the rest of the world. The rest of the world, except China, still at the time being shrouded in barbarism.

Some of these bored Khmtic types caravanned west to what is now Sierra Leone and took the westerly currents on papyrus boats and added to the cultures of Central and South America (The Olmecs); others walked right over Central America and changed the face of Easter Island forever, erecting gigantic Ramassede-type statues that looked toward Tanis. Still others sailed south and accelerated the technological development of Zimbabwe, building incredible Memphite fortresses from stone that could only have been found 1000 miles to the north. Others sailed north to Crete and started art and myth there. Some even sailed into Russia, India, Tibet, and China, retracing the route of Sesostris' I trek 500 years before and prefiguring Alexander's march 300 years later. In China and India they started a religion with a big, fat black sage as its center. And they were the ones who told the Chinese that if they wanted to preserve any vestige of Chinese culture, they'd better build one hell of a long, big wall to the west in a hurry.

But for the primary members of the royal family, these sort of excursions couldn't be. **HE** wouldn't allow it if he could help it. A pity in one large respect: relocated members of the royal family would have insisted that things be *written down on stone* to preserve the identities of those who did the thing. How could the Children of Aset have known that 2600 years later, people with uncombed, unstyled beards would be on the Discovery Channel claiming that Venusians or, at the very least, dislocated Europeans, built all the old monuments and started all world cultures? And how could the offspring of Asar have known sitting in the security of the Timeless Land that the predominant number of the uniquest of their unique protracted line 2600 years later, the African-Americans, would not only *not* know that they were descended from gods, but would also think that the only rock that could preserve them was crack? In the future time of such fair weather, crackheads could see everything clearly except themselves. How far one can fall when one doesn't know oneself.

But the royal family couldn't go or wouldn't go anywhere else cause they were home, and more, every day they got to stay within the presence of **HIM** and view his accomplishments. Tarharka's family—the Solar Blood— had it made in a world he had made for them.

Tarharka was the end result of the line of ruling Khmts who had decided that enough was enough up north, and it was time to reclaim the kingdom, make it the Land of the Blacks again instead of the Land of the Blacks and Semites (Why did you think it came to be called "The Two Lands" in the first place?). Before him, beginning with Kashta, would come Shabaka and Piankhy, and after him Tanutamon. Of course, the Semites would later become the Arabs and the Jewish and win in the end while they attempted to destroy each other. The 25th-Dynasty of Khmt would be its last native-ruled that *The New Columbia Encyclopedia* would recognize as black and African, even though that same text listed the native kings as "invaders from the south" and "Nubians" as though they were from another planet, and even though there were generations of Dynasties of the true rulers of Khmt continued to the south after the death of Tanutamon. After Tanutamon, the true Khmts would retreat to the south and rule from the new capitals at Napata and Meroe. But for the African moment, from the Mediterranean to Khartoum, and from the Lybian desert to the Ethiopian highlands, the Khmts—the blacks—ruled the greatest civilization that had ever been.

Why then had Tarharka now called an emergency meeting of the entire aristocratic class and the military from every province in the kingdom? He'd kicked Esarhaddon's ass so badly in 671 B.C. that the Assyrians wouldn't bug him for another 50 years. Peace treaties were all signed with the powerful neighbors, Libya, Nubia, Ethiopia, and no military might to the north was more than two sticks tied together. So what was up? But everyone knew they'd better be there or they'd have to go out and find real jobs.

* * *

"What happened? What went wrong?"

He stayed on his knees in the shadow of a column, gazed southeast and spoke aloud to himself in the largest place of worship ever built before or since, the Temple of the Sun at On (Karnak).

"I was feeling so good, everything goin so right … what's buggin my ass? Why can't I just relax like everybody else here and play in the sunshine?"

In the shadows, Tarharka searched through a portable porcelain carriage containing his 37,000 or so papyri. A corp of servants existed only to move that enormous carriage wherever Tarharka went and to exchange and remove papyri from the carriage to the library in Tanis. As he searched, 3 musicians strummed lyres.

"Hey! You 3. Cut that out now! Um only gonna tell you one more time, no more of that Khmtic urban stuff today. Um not in the mood. Only the latest fusion stuff from the country. Them Kushite brothers and sisters still know what time it is.

"I took on all the number 1 contenders and sent'em home with black eyes. I stuck a stella up in the middle of the damned Assyrian desert that they ride 20 miles out of the way just to avoid seeing. I hear the principle minority in Assyria, the Hebrews, have stuck me in some new pamphlet called the Pentateuch and called me more powerful than any Assyrian could hope to be, just to irritate the Assyrians. I'm re-doing all the principle monuments, this temple, the one down the mall there at Wa-set (Luxor), Ramses' million fucking statues spread out everywhere. I'll even put new lime-stone on the outside of the pyramids at Giza if I get the chance, so the Priesthood'll be happy, finally.

"The Army's got it better than any group of common citizens in the land. And the common folk know that as long as they work they'll eat and own property and no outsider can ever get close enough to them to take it away. We got the best schools in the world—except for those in Kush—and anybody who's got the money can go. We even let captured slaves marry into Khmt-hood if they stick around long enough.

"And the solar family has never been in better shape; I got five wives, 6 daughters and 6 sons—one for every sign in our Zodiac, not to mention enough uncles, aunts, nephews and other relative types enough to almost drive me out of my mind with their constantly wanting something just cause umma hit. If I croak tomorrow, they can start up another Pharaohnacy that they can trace all the way back to Amenhotep I (1570 B.C.) before um even cold. So if everybody is happy, why do I feel like tomorrow is Monday and I haven't slept all Sunday night?"

In the Temple of Ra he cheated. He revered Amon more and he couldn't help it. It was like trying to force Khmts to forget how to dance: you were what you were and that was that. The Sun God gave life to all things, but "The Hidden One" understood the unutterable secrets and stresses of what it meant to be African. Amon knew what it took to rule forever. So in the shadows he stayed, avoiding the rays of Ra, so that he might commune with a god who understood angst.

"Oh Amon, I am unworthy to even think your name, but I beseech you to bend like the sacred lotus to my supplication and tell me why um freakin out."

Nothing. Of course.

He lowered his head again and shouted at the walls.

"If only so many of my bourgeois brothers and sisters hadn't skipped town to `spread our culture.' Lazy cocksuckers. They just wanted to lay out in the sun and lord it over people who haven't even figured out how to eat without biting their fingers off. If I just had a royal brain-trust on this, I think things would be easier. But the priests have gotten so fundamentalist that they ain't even concerned about the things of this world anymore, and so many royal scholars left with the others that its hard to get up a quorum of academics. If it wasn't for our big library up north, I don't know how we'd keep up our educational standards. I'll just have to call the generals in. God, where is Amon when you need him?"

He spoke from the shadows to his guards to tell the generals to assemble in front of the two massive pylons he had erected at the front of the temple.

When Tarharka emerged from the temple, 100 of the smartest male and female military minds there had ever been lay prostrate before him on the burning cobblestones that stretched for half a mile. But their hamartia was their arrogance, and thus their belief that they could never be defeated, that they could never end, made them easy targets for those more hungry. Tarharka knew this, and it was why he had hesitated to consult situationally-molded intelligence made myopic by its own successes.

"HAIL MIGHTY TARHARKA, PHARAOH, KING OF KI—"

"Yeah, yeah, can all that shit ok. Let's get down to business. The reasons I called you all here are these. We got ourselves a couple of big problems that won't affect any of us here assembled. We'll be long dead before any of the stuff I don't want to happen happens. But unless we can come up with some answers, it's gonna happen, and there won't be no more Khmt."

The crowd murmured. This was the Timeless Land. There wasn't nothing before their ancestors except ice and dinosaurs. This was sacrilege the Pharaoh was mouthing, but nobody told Him to His face.

"This is the best place on earth, you all know that, and you know a house set on a hill cannot be hid, so everybody wants what we have. It's just non-Khmt human nature. We cannot sustain what we are if we get bored and arrogant. We cannot maintain what has been maintained since before there was a before if the best minds of our generation keep running away to plant our flags somewhere never to return. And you people and the priests have got to quit fighting over who is going to be the most privileged class. You're all living better than the common people, why are you so damned greedy? If you keep fighting among yourselves, the loyalties of the nation will be split and that'll be it. I can feel it.

"Furthermore, I don't expect the Assyrians to ever give up. Would you? Would you wanna try to make something grow in that damn desert they call home? Wouldn't you rather steal our art and sculpture than look at that ugly literal, one-dimensional stuff they pound together? Speaking of deserts, have you looked north lately at that big white thing coming this way from Libya at the rate of a foot a year? I'll give you one hint: that ain't snow folks and it ain't nothin nice. That's the Sahara, and by the time our grandchildren are adults, it'll be right under where your feet are now.

"Based on the technology we gave them, everybody else is developing new things and not telling us about them, new weapons, new devices. I just don't think we can continue to keep the whole world out of a place it wants to possess so bad. But as Khmts, as the Children of the Sun, we are bound to make sure that we live forever through our stones, culture, and children. We do this in our generation for the next, and they do it for the next, and so on. You all know it is not our way to live only for now.

"Next, this religion of ours is natural and powerful and it's sustained us for 3000 years, but it's got a fatal flaw as far as religions go: it's syncretic. Quit nodding your heads and rolling your eyes like you don't know what I mean. That crazy-ass Ihknaton comes up with Aton and we adopt it and believe in it for another thousand years. That right there is what I'm talking about. That's the way we are. If it helps, we're gonna keep it, enshrine it, make it holy. And while that's good news in the sense of spiritual growth for our **kas**, it is very bad news when that kind of absorptive religion meets a myopic one. Oh, there'll be a religion left after the battle. But trust me, it won't be nothing we can recognize as ours."

The head of Tarharka's calvary, General Principle, moved to the front of the crowd and cleared her throat to speak.

"Oh great Pharaoh, none shall ever undo us. We're the best things ever thought and everybody else trembles when they smell our perfume and cologne wafting across the sands."

"See, that's just the kind of attitude I'm talking about, complacent, ready to sit down, get fanned all day, and get fat. Are you forgetting that the Assyrians were just here a few years ago, and are you forgetting that they fight like monsters cause they ain't got no home worth going back to? They ain't like yall. They're hungry and afraid not to be that way. You must … think ahead. And don't forget, we ain't like them in another respect. We're a matriarchy. My sister in the armor over there, General Tenderoni, is as good as me and the family-line is carried through her, not me. When Khmtic women start having Assyrian babies, those babies are Khmtics. You get my drift?"

"Then what would you have us do O Pharaoh, you have but to command and—"

"Well, I was kinda hoping you well-paid career-military-personnel would help me on that. You know how I am: I always overdo or underdo, I can never get it quite right."

"No, Pharaoh is infallible and His word is the word of Amon-Ra, King of the Gods. What you say will be done."

"That's right, leave the whole thing up to me, then if I mess it up, you run back to your provinces and tell everybody I've been hitting the wine gourds too hard. It's getting hard to find a real Khmt these days.

"Alright, have it your way. Here's what I was thinking: we got to move to groove. Instead of everybody runnin off to Club Med like they been doin, let's send a *real* colony out to stay, one that carries with it every thing that we are and that we are not."

A wail went up form the entire group of assembled generals that could be heard for tens of miles. The servants screamed too and started to rend their clothing. Legends formed saying the wail could still be heard generations later reverberating off the walls of the Valleys of the Queens and Kings.

"Ok ok just wait a minute, let me finish. Amon, you blacks are emotional!

You think I like this idea? You think I wanna make these kinds of decisions? Anyway, we send out a gigantic colony with scholars, philosophers, masons, farmers, priests, soldiers, and servants. We give'em copies of every scroll we can locate in the entire kingdom, and we give'em enough gold and arms to start up a satellite kingdom when they get to where I'm thinking of. Now, in the Pyramid Texts of Hunefer, the scribe talks about a land—"

"No!" General Fallacy screamed, knowing that by interrupting the Pharaoh, he'd already occupied his tomb.

"Great Pharaoh, you ask too much of the people and of us! To disturb **IT** and ask some of us to leave sacred Khmt is too high a price to pay for your insecurities. I hear what everybody else has got to give up, including our ancestors, but I don't hear you giving up nothin!"

Those others nearest General Fallacy moved in to slice his head off, but Tarharka stopped them.

"Let me tell you something pal, anybody who's selected to go goes with his or her entire family. Am I getting through to you? *You* get to take Khmt with you, while I send with you … half my children."

No one could say a word. The man was obviously serious. But Solar Blood was pure. It had ALWAYS been so. You didn't dilute it and you didn't corrupt it. And you sure as hell didn't separate it from its heart.

"Now … like I was trying to say before, in the Pyramid Texts of Hunefer, the scribe writes about `the fertile land of Nok.' He says that before there were even Khmts that our ancestors, the Twa (little Kushites), went west and checked it out. They went west cause the Oldest People, the Tanzanians to the east where Africa ends, told them space was getting cramped and natural resources were getting tight, and it was time for some of the younger tribes to move on to more natural resources. The Oldest Ones are amazing: Words made Flesh because they're so logical and beautiful.

"When a small scouting party of Twa got out west, nobody could believe the news they brought back. They said if you dropped seeds on the ground they sprouted. Every drop of water was drinkable. To the north green hills full of game rolled on forever, and to the south and west fish jumped out of the Big Waters onto the land. And the place was weirdly spiritual—naturally possessed—like Khmt, but with not a soul around. Now the off-spring of that 5,000-year-old-Twa scouting party are still there. But they won't remember their cousins. They'll see us for the gods we are anyway if we show up there and probably roll out the red carpet.

"We send our people southwest. We can't go north. There's nothing there but the Mediterranean and barbarians. No culture. Some weak Greek theatre. Lotta Gauls and Teutons runnin around with animal skins on. Plus, it's cold, and you know how you blacks hate cold weather. We can't go west cause living in Libya would be just like living in the Sahara. We sure as hell can't go east cause out there the Assyrians are waiting to cut us into little bite-sized pieces. Besides, other than Libya, ain't none of them other places I mentioned Africa. We can't go southeast, cause that's Nubia and Kush and we don't disturb HOME. So I say we send them to Nok and they start Dynasty 26-B forever and ever Amon.

"Now, here's the hard part, the part I know you're all dreading. When the Old Man came up from down south and started the 1st Dynasty, as you all know he had **IT** constructed to honor his wife who was slain, fighting beside him, in the battles to reunite the Two Lands. He had **IT** buried 100 feet down at his city, Memphis. I don't have to tell you what that six-story sculpture of solid gold represents, what it means.

"Menes consecrated that beautiful, solid-gold woman to contain all of our spirits. She is Khmt and Khmt is She. As long as She survives, Khmt survives."

"And you would send her way from us!" they all screamed, caught between Pharaoh and Prophecy, and thus, not being able to do anything except scream and tear off their own ears.

"No, you're right. Don't be stupid. She's larger than the Sphinx and you know he molded Her standing, eyes looking back Home. There's no way to move something like that through the Sahara and into Nok 1200 miles away. We must always survive. But survival at the cost of Her is too much to pay for perpetuity. No, we don't send Her, but we send … a part of Her.

"General Tenderoni, you get up three or four divisions and assemble back here in an hour. When you get back I'll give you some sealed orders of what to do when you reach the end of the assigned march at Memphis. You—you must follow those orders implicitly no matter how you feel about them when you see them. I am Pharaoh and you are Pharaoh's sister as well as a general in the royal army. We are Solar. We are one. We are both the Children of Ra."

Tarharka looked away from her toward the group, tears in his eyes.

"The rest of you will now do exactly what I instruct. You will return to your 30 Nomes. In one month you will meet General Tenderoni and me in Memphis. You will have with you your 100 best representatives from the groups I named before. They must be volunteers and they must be told that they will not be allowed to return home. Remind them that they are Khmtic and that they are bound by their existence to ensure that they exist forever. When you assemble in Memphis during the Feast of the Bull God Apis,

I… I-I will give final instructions to everyone concerned. Remember the power of Amon and tell no one except those concerned. I know the priesthood will try to have my ass for this, but that's the way it is."

To show that his audience was finished, Tarharka crossed both fists across his massive chest, tinkling, clanging, and shining all over, his arms touching at the forearms, with a silver flail in one hand and a solid gold ankh in the other. The generals fell to their bellies again and repeated the sacred verses of reverence. Then they rose as one and began to depart.

Tarharka stared at the back of his sister as she stopped, turned and stared back to look at him, not being able to see him clearly because he had again backed into the shadows.

She blinked and turned away. It must have been the tears in her eyes. For a moment, she had thought she saw a ram's head beneath the shadow of the column.

Chapter 14

Z ip:

"Like I said, there's nothing here. I hope you ain't lookin for some kinda physical sign to have lasted this long. Cause if you are, we may as well try to conjure up old Menes and get him to tell us. Cause ain't shit left here that ain't been overturned. Every possible thing that could remind the South that it lost gets bulldozed, buried or rewritten except the big houses, weapons, flags, and the plantation-mentality left to blacks."

As the sun's top arc remained barely visible to the west above the tin roof of the car wash, Siedah attacked her HewlettPackard and cross referenced her displays with the local map.

Dennis rubbed the bricks of the hardware store, rubbed the curb of the sidewalk, stood in the middle of Haynes, and then turned toward Siedah. "What are you doin with that thing now. We're here already."

"No, not exactly. Hold on. It's runnin."

"That way," she shouted, pointing south, "about 200 yards. Let's go babies."

* * *

All three of the fortune hunters stood silent facing the old, two-story structure, recently a frat-house, then abandoned, and now turned into a church. But they were staring over and around the structure at the woods.

Zip whispered, "This is it … I can feel it … I … this is it. Ain't no doubt about it."

There was enough light to avoid stumbling over the dead tree limbs, bicycle parts, and beer empties, but just enough. Over the whole place hung an air of murder and mystery and the sweet smell of the supernatural. This place screamed out to them to do … something.

Now deeply into the woods behind the church, Dennis was amazed. Siedah stared at the calculator.

"Now *this* is exactly where the treasure was put on the plantationat least, this is as exact to the spot as I can figure from the calculator."

"How can woods like these exist a few yards from civilization? I mean, we just passed a school back there, and now here we are in a grown over national park," whispered Dennis, and then he dropped to his knees and began to dig frantically.

Zip spoke up, "This is Memphis baby. *My* home. We zone for race, not for logic."

"What are you doing Dennis?" Siedah put her hand on her 24" waist and stared down.

"Just dig Zip, Siedah, both of you, dig. Get that broken hoe over there, anything. Look, this is the edge of a part of the foundation right here, and it's less than a foot down. Come on dig goddamit. Start at three different angles 30 feet apart and work toward the center of the triangle. Those are about the dimensions that were on those plans, right Siedah?"

But she couldn't hear him. She was throwing leaves and dirt and beer bottles so spasmodically that she heard nothing. This was a new life they were digging up from this scorched and dead plantation. She could hear all Dennis had to say after the Mutual Funds receipts were in the safety deposit box.

* * *

Thirty minutes and two and a half feet down later as they converged toward the center of the triangulation of the long vanished greatroom, one of Zip's gold rings hit something metal.

"Oh it's gotta be GOLD!" screamed Dennis, throwing mounds of mud and decayed leaves into the air to reveal the edges of more metal.

"Dennis, this is metal, but it's not gold. Just chill out will you. Maybe this is like the top of a chest or something." The workout had sobered Siedah from her frenzy. Zip threw dirt to trace the edges of the metal and spoke.

"Well, it's something. Come on. It curves down this way, and then out. It's got some kind of mold shape to it on this side. Feel's mighty strange."

A few more minutes of feverish tossing, and these three children of the present South dropped their hands simultaneously and gasped.

"It's the ..." Dennis couldn't get it out.

" ... top of some kind of ... " Siedah, out of breath, stammered.

" ... some kind of ... head." Zip wiped dirt out of his eyes and kept right on digging.

Dennis turned to Siedah. "Are you thinking what I'm thinking? That stuff in the Jones' manuscript about the bought brass never used, gone when the house was opened up to the regular slaves and guests. They—"

"They smelted some precious metal right here in the house those nights when three of the favorites stood at the unfinished doors with rifles and knives. They smelted it and then they" Dennis cut Siedah off.

"The other three poured it into a mold they had shaped with their own hands and buried it underneath the floor of the great room. It's probably Jefferson Davis' head. DisneyWorld needed icons. That's why Winchester poisoned those 6 `favorite' slaves under the pretense of giving them liquor for a job well done! Lucinda never knew why her cousins and uncles were murdered, or by whom, because those who passed the story down never knew the truth ... only Winchester knew."

Zip looked up from the hole.

"Hey, this ain't no Charlie Chan movie; I don't need you to reconstruct the crime. Will you get your asses down here and help me dig? I am not intended for manual labor."

"And Winchester had every intention of coming back and digging up the head, Siedah, but his cowardice undid him," Dennis spoke, trying to hide his disgust.

"And to think those slaves took that honkie in and bathed him and fed him, and bandaged his cuts when he came crawling back through the Federal lines ... " Siedah shook her head.

Zip spoke from beneath the bottom of the nose of the head.

"Siedah, don't let what other people did or do make you act like them. This whole ugly script ain't got nothing to do with hating white people. But it's got everything to do with loving yourself. Don't misunderstand me. I forgive everybody everything, but I ain't forgettin nothin ... I don't know why um sayin all this. This place has a strange effect on me. But money don't love nothing but itself Siedah. It might be a good thing for us three urban professionals to remember. Now, will somebody please get on your knees and, like, pretend that you wanna get this head out? If it's fulla diamonds or something, there's no way in hell I can lift it."

But Dennis and Siedah were too shocked to move. From what Zip had already uncovered, it was obvious that Jefferson Davis' head had never looked like that. It was was the head of a Khmt, a sister from way back! Ha! Ha! Ha! This was the biggest joke of all on Millbranch. Where had he been when the slaves quickly fashioned the brass and lowered the head into the hole in the great room floor? Probably out back, forcing his way into doing what a well-read librarian years later would deny any antebellum white gentleman capable of doing. Dennis and Siedah dived into the hole and began scraping dirt.

Finally, 8 feet down and 8 across, their fingers felt the jagged bottom of the base of the head.

"Ok, Siedah, drag that 2 x 4 over here, and Dennis and I will lever it up. Then you push dirt up under it. We'll keep doing that til we get it up level, and maybe we can drag it outta here before its completely dark."

* * *

Completely dark. Completely and totally black. I mean, opaque.

That's what the scene was when they got to what they figured to be their last stop in this very strange tour of the South, in this, the middle of the second term of President Oprah Winfrey's United States.

There had been no need for the Ziplaborate plans of levering he'd stolen from that movie *The Egyptian* and I.E.S. Edwards' book *The Pyramids of Egypt*; when he and Dennis had pushed their full weight down on the 2 x 4, the head shot out of the trench like a champagne cork.

"Shit," Zip was heard to characteristically say as he struck the base of the now sideturned head with the 2 x 4, "Listen to that echo. It tolls for yalls' asses. It's as empty as Dennis' head. What am I doin here? Look at my jumpsuit."

Closer examination by Dennis only confirmed Zip's fears. The eightfoot head of a Khmt was empty. Empty like Zip's pockets; hollow like Dennis' hopes.

Someone had moved to some unknown spot all that Winchester had so elaborately hidden; he, building his great room and burying his treasure at a mathematical bisection before solar-operated calculators were even thought of. It wouldn't matter if everything were burned down around the place, wouldn't have mattered if gigantic buildings were on top of it; that head could always be pinpointed right under the middle of the great room by anyone who figured out the riddle of the bisecting lines and could do basic math. And now it was gone. Dennis and Zip stood in the muddy hole, hands on hips, staring down. Only Siedah continued to glare at the head.

Dennis dropped to his butt and bawled. "This is what my life has come too; looking for buried treasure, outta work, all my library books overdue

... I-I'd rather read ten black novels on November 22 than go through this kinda torture."

"Look Dennis, it's not your fault. It was a chance. Takin a chance is always better than standin still and ... wishing ... I didn't have to leave Mr. Hugh and come with you. It was a chance to do quick what um gonna do slow and right now. You can come with me. You can be my manager. Um gonna need a manager ... now"

"Kiss my ass. Um gonna roll right over in this hole and die as soon as I bust this head wide open."

Dennis snatched the 2 x 4 from Zip and started trying to crawl out of the muddy hole. As he grabbed the ridge, Siedah screamed.

"Wait! Dennis, don't touch that head. You and Zip put it back in the hole just the way it was, *exactly* the way it was."

"Siedah, give it up willya?" Dennis slobbered through his tears, "It's over. It's through. Give it up."

"No. Goddamit put that head back in the hole like I tell you!" screamed Siedah.

Zip helped Dennis to his feet. Zip already knew there was no point in arguing with Siedah. She was too much like him. They pushed the head back into the hole, and then, pushing against the side of the left nostril, managed to turn it back to its original position.

"Ok, there it is. Now what does that prove?" Dennis was completely disillusioned.

"Oh my god! Look at the eyes will you?"

"What the hell about em? They're eyes. That's it. Khmtic eyes."

"No. Look at them again." Siedah jumped into the narrow opening between the earth and the eyes.

"Those eyes are glaring at something. The paint's all gone from them now I know, but the balls are still molded up and to the sides. Look where they're looking! What direction is that Zip? The sun's so far down, I can't get my bearings."

"It's south."

"And which way was the odd beam facing Dennis, the 90?"

"East. What are you trying to say?"

"I don't know. Maybe them slaves weren't as altruistic as we thought. Maybe, just maybe, if we keep the repetition of the number eight in our minds, eight beams, seven at thirty three and a third, one absurdly ninety, the one designed personally by Menes no doubt, pointing directly east; eight beams; seven plus one is eight. Just maybe if we go sixteen miles southeast, directly toward New Orleans, we might find a treat that those slaves made for us at the expense of Winchester. That treasure had to go somewhere."

"Ms. Sherlock Holmes, I don't mean to bust your bubble, but sixteen miles southeast of here will put your fine ass right in the middle of Big Muddy." Zip tried not to laugh, he tried not to cry, but it was all so ridiculous, this whole escapade, that he let out a couple of Shango screams and then did something he only did when extremely depressed and there was no one around; he started rapping:

> *"A brother can't do nothin no more/*
> *They give'im the key*
> *but move the fuckin door/*
> *What's next, what's next, for my black ass?/*
> *If this is life, I think I'll pass."*

"Then I guess that 16's not the number." Siedah murmured without looking at Zip.

"But Zip," Dennis was coming back to himself, squeezing his hands where the brass of the head had turned the wood of the 2 x 4 into a handshatterer, "where does 8 miles put us, 8 miles southeast?"

"It … I don't know. I don't give a damn. Somewhere in south Memphis. *' What's next, what's next …* '"

"Zip's gone somewhere else Siedah. Let's put him the car and head southeast."

"First let's bury the dead," she said, and Siedah threw the first hoefull of dirt back into the hole. "Dennis, hmmph, push it—push it til the eyes are pointing farther southeast that they were before. Good, just a little bit more. That's it. Roughly straight across the Atlantic Ocean. She's waited for ages to do her job, and she's done it for us. Let her finally look at the Land of the Ages. Let her look at … home."

* * *

After a stop in the allnight convenience store at the corner for shovels:

"This is *not*, I repeat *not* my fucking idea of fun Dennis. Do you know what time it is?"

"It's midnight Zip."

"Right, and what night of the week is it?"

"It's Friday night Zip."

"Uh huh, that's right! That's right! Friday night! Goddamn I hate Friday nights in Memphis! Now, do you also know what area this is we're standing in with shovels in our hands?"

"Yes, Zip, its a graveyard."

"'Yes, Zip it's a graveyard.' No Dennis. It's a fucking GRAVEYARD!!! A graveyard, do you understand? Me, an urban partyboy and deepthinker, in a graveyard in the middle of the night, thinking about digging into the dirt. Uh. This is it brother. You keep the goddamed treasure or whatever it is. I am taking my ass back to the car and back home. Um gonna retire from this thing called LIFE. I'd like to retire. Digging up graves no longer amuses me. I think I'll devote my remaining years to trying to balance the federal budget. Y'know, something quiet and easy."

"Don't nutup on me Zip. This is it. I can feel it this time …"

Siedah called from the middle of the graveyard. "It's here. Oh my God! I found it. Over here."

The old stone marker read:

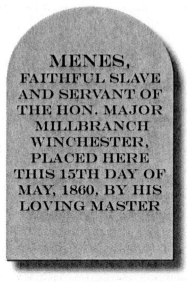

MENES,
FAITHFUL SLAVE
AND SERVANT OF
THE HON. MAJOR
MILLBRANCH
WINCHESTER,
PLACED HERE
THIS 15TH DAY OF
MAY, 1860, BY HIS
LOVING MASTER

"Ooo Zippeee! This is it! This is it!" Siedah screamed.

In spite of his better judgment, Zip raced right behind Dennis, skinning his legs on old tombstones and metal flowerpot holders, here, in this graveyard, at the corner of Elvis Presley Blvd. and Elliston.

He knew the area. Knew all the public stories, and the stories that were run down the black grapevine, and he knew some stories that not even the local paper nor the more reliable grapevine knew. Knew that down Elliston they had just razed the Victorian house where, until recently, the retired local school teacher kept her unbalanced daughter, driven insane by being crucified on a cable spindle and having both breasts cut off by the Chicago Political Machine in the late '30s. The daughter had thought that Chicago was a haven of liberal thought when she typically, teacherly, said on live radio that the city government was purposely sending damaged and out-of-date books to the city's black schools and siphoning off funds from the small black school board's allotments to put in local, white politicians' pockets. Had named names right there on live radio. After all, this wasn't Memphis, where she was from, where in the late '20s her mother had instilled in her the spiritual gift of good teaching, and where that same Phi Beta Kappa mother was relegated to one of the only two black public schools in Memphis at the time and paid half what white female teachers were paid. The mother, who, even with that Phi Beta Kappa key and degrees from Fisk and Harvard under her belt, still had to use the colored restroom at the back of the Woolworth's off Main. No, hell, this was Chicago. UP NORTH. Every educated and uneducated black from downhome was runnin up north where **EVERYTHING WAS BETTER!** Sure it was better. Anything had to be better than the south, right?

And then they crucified her and cut her breasts off, and until recently she had occasionally escaped from the house to try to bum cigarettes and show that she had on no underwear.

And he knew that farther down Elliston, just before it curves toward its end at the L & N railroad tracks, was the man they called Walking Dead; the one who could throw bricks around corners and who did the same atrocity to anyone, male or female, old or young, he caught alone in the graveyard at night. "The old stones speak when Dead come walking by," said old folks in the shot-gun houses to the south of the graveyard.

And he knew that his best friend as a teenage boy used to take his dates to this graveyard and they'd screw on the stones. John called it "raising the dead." Zip called it fucking crazy, which is what he felt like right now, because even with all he knew, his feet kept going toward Siedah and the ... IT ... and anything different than what he had known before. And he couldn't stop them.

* * *

Standing over the grave of Menes, wind rushing, trees rustling, every loose piece of paper making "smack" sounds as they struck the cold stones, Zip's being was flooded with images of greed, betrayal, and murder. He just couldn't figure it out because he was trying to listen to his head again, his logic, and REAL LIFE, not that shit he read in the paperbacks and watched on CineMax, always defied logic.

REAL LIFE defied all logical reasoning because it was all murder, senselessness, exploitation, and pressure-packed actions in the face of an overwhelming lack of money and certain death. How in the hell could you impose a grid of logical response over human beings when the only logic the strong ones knew was to eat up the weak ones, and the only logic the weak ones knew was to have more children for the strong ones to eat? His answer was to sing about love as passionately and as logically as he could. Others turned to dope, some to the more intoxicating religion, and as a show of their hatred for being born in the first place, the worst of them all simply devoured each other physically, emotionally, and spiritually not forgetting to remove the cash from the suckers' pockets first.

And he couldn't figure out what he, personally, him, Zip Ingentry Peters, was doing here in a graveyard, far from his tapes and synthesizer, with the anthropormorphose of everything that was good, smart and sexy already pushing the tip of her spade into the leaf-covered mound, and with the personification of unrewarded genius, who stared down past his blond lashes at the mound as though in a trance. How could he, Zip, be standing here, shovel in hand, loathing one ancestor and loving another, whose bones he was about to displace because those bones might be lying on top of a fortune? Nevertheless:

"Let's do it to it!" Zip shouted, and stabbed his spade into the small mound.

Dennis and Siedah plunged their shovels in with all the enthusiasm that the ownership of talents, shekels, gold, money, Geld, capital, bread, ducats, ends, filthy lucre engenders, sweating, slinging blades of earth and leaves into the late July night air.

Siedah knew she was dirtier at that precise moment than she'd ever been, all told, of her 38 years, her sweat turning the flying dirt into mud soon after it came to rest on the shoulders, chest, and thighs of her Dior aerobics suit. Tonight she knew a lot of things.

"This was far more than I thought, more than I was asking for. Everybody gets bored, life being what it is. This ZipMan is what I need right now, what works for me right now, and I always do what works for me. When I dreamed him up, I hadn't thought about the money, but shit, what's the use of having a hotdog with no bread? We take this gold or whatever it is, turn it over in Switzerland, borrow against it in the Bahamas, put the cash in plastic vials in our little pussies and boodies, and head out. See the world on cash fore they blow it up. Get back home to Southland, build the floorsafe ourselves, buy money orders every month to recycle the cash, and keep a low local profile til we're dead. Oh! Trips, jewelry, sculpture, a Nautilus, groceries for our poor relatives, and French food and French wine every night at Antoine's! It's almost as sweet as being in love. Almost.

"Ooo! That man singing to me, in a hot tub, and long hot waves and streams of joy forever, just like back at my condo on my desk. If it don't last forever, he can take his half of the cash and the memories and the technostuff, and I'll take mine. The duty for self-fulfillment goes on long after great sex has become standard." And, of course, as a fail-safe, she'd kept Earl's number.

And Dennis:

"No more deadend jobs that you train thirty years to get and then lose in two semesters through no fault of your own. No more hobo clothing. No more pompous, tenured assholes. No more excuse-filled, poor excuses for students. No more burning my eyes out grading so-called college-level essays written at about the same level as I wrote when I was seven. No more reading criticism that reads like it was written by a chimp and translated by an orangutan on Jack Daniels. No more fighting for parking spaces at 7 a.m. No more two classes at 8 & 9 in the morning and two more at 8 & 9 at night. No more listening to my little punk nephew tell me over and over how he, with no degree in anything, makes twice as much money at his BurgerBomb management job as I do with four degrees and twenty-seven years of teaching. No more self-delusions that dedication to teaching poor students and a commitment to scholarly excellence are more important

than penny stocks, junk bonds, and 9% interest on apartment complexes.
NOMORENOMORENOMORE!

About a foot down, after all the leaves and twigs and dry topdirt had
been shoveled to the side, Zip saw another layer of dried leaves mixed in and
totally unlike the rich, moist, black dirt he'd been throwing into the wind.
He turned to Siedah, his mouth open.
"What the fu—"
And then the clouded light from the full moon went out.

* * *

And he fell and he fell and he fell up into the darkness, the blackness,
until he landed headfirst onto a vast opaque plane. All around was only
blackness, and he was freezing in it, suffocating in it, not knowing what to do
as he looked around with no apparent reflection in sight; nothing knowable
from which to get a sense of himself. He extended his invisible right hand in
first one direction and then the next direction and shivered in loneliness: his
base seemed to be only a pod beyond whose edges was nothing.
Shaking, convulsing in the cold, the emptiness, he fell backward onto his
back, flinging his arms up in resignation. And then his right hand brushed
something warm.
Extending his right hand above his head, he knew immediately the
warmth had a human source. But the tops of its feet were smooth as jade
and its ankles were hard and taut.

From roughly 6 feet above him two small beams of light streamed out
onto the left side of his chest from the form's head. And then he could barely
see the outline of the source's form: perfect, majestic, never-before-known,
and darker even than the blackness which surrounded him.
Behind the source was a black door, locked, with an enormous black
padlock protruding from the fastening hinge. The lock was as large as a
person. Through the crevices of the door, incredible warmth and sweet
smells issued; and he knew, somehow, that behind the door was not only
safety, but everything he had always wanted to know: what his world was,
why his world was, and the sweet secret, the unutterable secret to conquering
that world.
But the lock:

Gigantic.

Indestructible.

And, then, from the form, a laser-like, illuminating smile. And in its left hand, a black key.

* * *

The gigantic tumblers turned as though they were weightless. And as the form pulled wide the door, Zip was permeated by a blast of rushing black light, which illuminated everything and burned his skin from his body, leaving him scorched and blacker than it had ever been before.

And then he lay nude on the beach at Gulfport, the north star glaring in his tear-filled eyes, and the form, ineffably drifting over the roaring waves ceaselessly toward him.

Chapter 15

When Zip opened his eyes, the first thing he saw was Menes' tombstone above his head. And the first thing he felt was whiteheat pain in the very top of his skull.

"Shiiit!" Zip screamed, giving up the grave, and then the pain pushing him to his knees, again to lean his arm on the tombstone.

"Si! Siii!" But she didn't answer. Eyes still blurry, equilibrium gone too, he could still make out that there were no shadows or shapes standing in the cemetery. Just the wind and the moon and him and then he saw the white Addidas jutting from behind another tombstone.

"Glurr, blrppt, sonsabitches, bastards, graverobbers ... Siedah ..."

"Dennis, Dennis," Zip shaking him at the shoulders, "you ok? You ok?"

"I'm not gonna make it ... ooo ... my head ... my brains are running out ..."

Zip blurrily rubbed his hand through Dennis' dirty, blond hair, feeling his hand filled with blood and tissue as he pulled it back toward his clouded eyes.

"Zip, um not gonna make it ... but look ... they, they grabbed Siedah and dragged her toward the truck. They hadn't counted on her being as strong as she is ... their bodies'll remember her fists, knees, nails, teeth. I'll tell you that; she kicked the shit out ofem... Glurt."

"Dennis be quiet now. I gotta drag you to— ooh my head— to the phone booth at the corner and call the police. Ow!"

"No. Forget that. Just listen ..."

He rubbed his hand through Dennis' head again. Now Zip had a wild look of surprise on his face.

"Two guys, blond anna black, forty-ish, big bellies, eyes close together ... FineMart pants, thick shoes, the smell of Black Jack and Pabst ... y'know, typical Fans ... grabbed her, into the pickup ... drove out headin east toward Elvis Presley ... Zip, in the back, a sheet covering something wide and tall ..."

"Think it was whatever was originally in the head?"

"Ohhh ... don't know, but coulda been ... don't play around with these boys ... handled Siedah likea dog ... now call the police ..."

"Come on. I got to get you up. Can't call the cops. Enough low-class people seem to know about ... umph ... this whole enterprise already. Owww!" Zip shakily stood to his feet. His head pounded as the world spun around. He started to drag Dennis by the armpits toward Elliston.

"Zip don't be a damn fool ... leave me, hurry, call cops ... Siedah more important than the treasure, more important than anything."

Zip said nothing as Dennis' Addidas heels hit the asphalt. Over Zip's shoulder, the neon light from the Fina station red, white and bluely illuminated the two struggling shadows.

"Zip, that girl loves you whether you know it or not, you asshole ... and you love her ... why is it so hard for you to face the fact that you might need somebody ... too important to throw away ... geter back ... Zip, I gota sister in Macon ... Lisa Todd ... caller, teller what happened, teller sorry I couldna done something worthwhile with my life ... and you Zip ... you didn't have to complicate your life with me ... I love you too ... I'll be lookin down on you ... ohhh ..."

"Umph ... Dennis, itsa flesh wound ... that was mud in my hand before... umph... why don't you take off a few professorial pounds ... you not gon die fool. You... umph... exagerratin ..."

"I know ... but um tryin to make a ..."

* * *

"Sometimes at night as the wind and the rain come through the pines umma boy again, among the migrant pickups, and um finally home. The thing that bothers me the most is that I was unable to share with them all that I would eventually become. Admittedly, in my own mind that ain't much, but to them it woulda been like Ricky Ricardo showing up in the fields to buy an apple. But, god, first she went, and then he ... and I never was able to show them my thanks for making me.

"I have zero idea why poor people would think that they have some god-given right to have children when the only people who are going to suffer for the parents' dumbness are the very children they think they have a right to have; and I have zero idea why once these poor people have one child they'd want to have another and another and another; and I have zero idea why after these kids from moneyless, powerless, usually semi-literate families start discriminating against the kids of other poor parents at their jobs, start burning out their noses with PCP, and beating each other and their own poor kids for reasons they can't even begin to figure out—why they all think that it's only their own faults that every thing about them is doomed and deadly because of them. The stupid parents die scott-free, and the kids repeat the cycle so that they can die scott-free.

"I have zero idea about the *whys* of these things, yet even I have to admit that um an intellectual in all the truest and worst definitions of that awful yellowstar label and that I ought to be able to figure those things out, since not only am I overly-bright, but am also the end, last, and best product of two such semi-literate parents, but all I can do is shake my head at their lost memories and all the stupid parents like them, and go kiss their dual image in the mirror cause um so glad to be alive instead of nothing.

"If I just coulda moved a little faster—but I moved like lightening and it still wasn't fast enough. I made some tremendous something out of less than absolutely nothing, and it all still amounted to nothing in my own mind because by the time I had made awful, poor, white-trash, backgroundless nothing into semi-something, they were both just … just gone.

"Mama was already gone and I don't remember much about her except the emptiness, the not seeing or feeling that warm and familiar force around anymore. But when Thomas went—I always called him Thomas, I don't know why—I was 7, and I perceived death the only and best way I could I guess; it was like, you have access to someone you love, and maybe that access is only a long-distance call every week, but you need that call every week like you need air: desperately; and then someone—I don't know who, god, the phone company—but someone disconnects the line and you can never, ever talk to that person again that you desperately need to talk to. And that was death to me.

"Now that I know the real ins and outs of death—plutonium ugliness as only 19th-century Russian writers can portray it—none of that stuff is as real or depressing to me as my childhood image of death being that disconnected telephone line. And here, some sixty years later, I still wish I could climb a pole and reconnect those lines.

"The most ironic and funniest part of this is that your parents almost always see things in the exact opposite way that you do. I remember after I got my first job. I had a little money, had worked doubles through the Thanksgiving and Christmas holidays, and I went back to Savannah and got all the siblings together. I was gonna re-cement the family with this party. I was gonna fuse the blood through all the offspring of Thomas and Emy Johnston.

"After 5 minutes together in that Sparkling Inns suite, if a single one of us had a gun with enough bullets we would have shot all the others' brains out without a single thought. I mean we were not only different in age and temperament, we hated each other with a savage ferocity because of our differences that I've only read about between the Khmts and Assyrians. I mean, we wanted to wipe each other out because we were locked in one room together and forced to pretend that blood was thicker than our own failings. And since I was the one who came up with the whole idea, the rest of'em blamed it all on me. And goddamit, I deserved it.

"While I was backing into a corner looking for a handy blunt instrument, I realized that my parents would have laughed themselves into convulsions—*were* laughing themselves silly somewhere in Parent Heaven. And I remembered that Thomas and Emy had always seen us for what we so disappointingly were: They knew this one over here was a loser, that one over there ugly, that this one here was likely to become a murderer, and that one there was born with the IQ of a gnat. They judged their children for what they were individually and treated them accordingly, and here I was going to make us all into Andy Hardy and the Cosby Kids in three hours with wine and cheese and a few b/w photos.

"So I learned that all I could speak for in front of my parents' spirits was myself, and that there I was at 60 years of age able to interpret whole volumes at a single bound, but that I still couldn't spare the money for two tombstones for my parents' graves.

"When I found what I found doing what I usually did after working all day, I knew it was my last chance, the only way to prove to me that I could show their spirits that I did not have to pay my whole life through for just two mistakes—the mistake of being born to poor parents and the mistake of choosing the wrong profession.

"Thomas would probably say, `Oh Dennis, this is good enough. We're dead. What you are is more than good enough and more than we ever dreamed of being or dreamed that any of our kids would ever be.'"

Dennis' synapses continued to try to pulsate linearly through his busted-open, bleeding, throbbing skull.

"But … but umon tell yall something folks. In the same way that I have zero idea why poor people have children, I know with 100% certainty why I gotta find that boy and **IT**. This time I win my way, or I come join you. Either way … I win."

* * *

"You! You! I shoulda goddamit known! Behind the scenes. Just like Mrs. Jones wrote: 'White folks' dirt is cleaner than it used to be.'"

Silently peering through its covering sheet and through the back window of the pickup, a gigantic, mute Khmt head observed Jim Rawlins, Siedah's supervisor at NEGCO, and Roland Lafayette, a thousandnaire via his father's coinop washerettes ("PASS-N-WASH") and thereby an entrepreneur. His latest escapade, which had gotten him the Baton Rouge Black Businessman of the Year Award, had been to build an antebellum restaurant, as recently the country had turned even more to astigmatically look backward rather than face anything that had to do with the ugliness of the present of which they were a part. Hell, always give the people what they want.

And he was going to surround them with the contrived past: meek, darky waiters in white jackets, banjo music for entertainment, and Southern singalongs in the rotunda of the bar. "Dixie" and "The Tennessee Waltz" would be favorites. Maybe even invite Governor Whoopi Goldberg (now in her 12th term) down from time to time to wear a Confederate uniform and rub elbows.

Hell, it didn't matter if Lafayette, himself, was a darker Negroid than most present-day Kenyans. The point was to get as rich as possible by cheating shut-out blacks and licking the rim of every white ass-hole he could find, and in a minute he'd be county assessor—or even mayor—and the white boys who put his black ass there in the first place could get on TV and talk about how racially advanced they had become and what a great job their Sambo was gonna do, and then they could ride to state senator or governor on their magnanimity, and Mr. Lafayette's children could have Mercedes and Jeeps while still in their teens and he would always have friends in white places, and even when he died, with his pallbearers, the mayor and the senator eyeing his widow's ass, Lafayette would still be in the black. Oh, how the world had changed course since the '65 Civil Rights Act.

But Mr. Lafayette didn't know that waiting for him, staring from behind Asar's scales, was a smiling and volcanic Tarharka.

And how could Lafayette have known, this dufus's highest intellectual achievement being his decision to add chlorine to his mansion's pool in Baton Rouge, that by flipping through a book called *Ghosts Along the Mississippi* 3 weeks before, he'd come across a photograph of a mansion said to be the finest ever constructed in Memphis; that after hiring an architectural/ engineering firm to research and draw up the plans, that a certain official at NEGCO would call him and tell him that some mighty mysterious stuff was happening with that research and the nigger he'd assigned to do the task, and maybe they'd better keep in touch and stay abreast of what was going on with the work on the "Winchester Place" restaurant?

And how could Lafayette have known that the whole mess would end up in the summer of 2020 and lead to this night in July when he would pull a eightfoot, gold nigra head out of another nigger's grave, bop yet another nigger and a Georgia fruit on the head, and be confined in a pickup cab with a wild woman, who, even now, thinking Zip dead, was threatening to ignore the .38 he had poked into her ribs and stick her long fingernails through his eyeballs?

"You just cool out now baby. Hey Jim, we shoulda just knocked her in the head too! She's too much trouble."

"No. I wanna talk to her just a minute. Now Si, you and me, we understand each other, we're just alike."

"Fuck you."

"Yeah, well, gimme time. Been wantin do to that for years anyway. But what um gettin at is that you and me, we understand how the world really is. It ticks on power and money, and as long as you understand that and don't tamper with the mechanism, well, it won't blow up in your face. Now being a smart girl like yourself, um sure you can see the efficacy of us comin together on our little secret. Now, Mr. Lafayette over there, he wants to git him a little piece and then blow your head off, or maybe viceversa, but I've gotten him to cool down a minute if you and me can come to terms. We give you $50,000 cash and you forever forget all about Africans and Winchesters and ninety degree angles. Forever. You understand what um sayin?"

"Yeah, I speak English. That don't mean umon do it though. You some tough guys with your guns and when you sneakin up behind people with shovels. Why don't you tell your girlfriend to put his pistol down and we'll just fight for the conclusion of this story. Let the best ending win?"

"Oh come on Si. Grow up. Look to your right. Every onea you Negroes has got your price. What would it take? Ain't there *something* I can do for you?"

"Yeah, there is something you can do for me. Back behind curvaceous me, just below my waist, is a hard-to-get-to spot that's never been kissed;

now, um gonna bend over, and what I want you to do with all the gusto you can muster is—"

"—why don't we just poper now Jimmy? She's drivin me crazy. Goddam I wish I had blown her head off in the graveyard!"

"Is that your final answer Si? You sure you know whatchu doin?"

"That's just like you Fans. You all want the REAL TRUTH from real people so you can figure out how to hurt them with something you otherwise have no experience with. Well, nobody gets that from me. But you can have this."

HOOEEEBRRRTTTT! Siedah stretched her head down as close to her ankles as possible and ripped an enormous, cacophonous gaseous explosion into the sealed cab of the pick-up. As Mr. Lafayette jerked her up by her hair with his right hand and fanned his face with his left hand, Siedah hurled sweet saliva into the distracted driver's face. The spit in his face was final confirmation of the surety of Siedah's initial answer, as the truck's driver, shocked, gassed, and blinded, swerved and ran into the shins of the statue of the "Great Public Benefactor," his bronze head falling and crushing the cab of the truck, as another, much larger head, never 'lowed in the history of Memphis books, catapulted out of the truck bed, rolled, and came to rest upright over the cup of the 9th Green, again facing southeast.

Even the sedated seniors of nearby Parklane Rest Home were awakened by the rippling explosion of the gasoline tank.

Chapter 16

"I just couldn't see the big picture before/
Now I know the way to go that I never knew/
I never knew/
But that picture ain't got no frame/
Without your face in my life/
Can't believe that it's over now/
It just don't seem right/
And I can't make life's video without your love."

"And so this is what I've come to," the ZipMan thought as he stumbled through downtown Memphis toward Front Street, "looking at the uneven blocks of the MidAmerica Mall through tears, no Siedah, no Dennis, no treasure, no job, no nothin. Right back where I started, except worse off. It's days like this you ask yourself what your parents coulda been thinkin when they decided or made a mistake and gave you a starting place in the gate."

Up 3 nights running now, since the crazy man had pulled his tuxtails in Atlanta, through Memphis, back to Atlanta, the blind luck of love in New Orleans, back to Memphis, through the mud and tombstones and into the park last night, Zip tried to rewind and slomo everything in sequence through his head, but he was so tired and depressed.

* * *

"Well what hospital did you take the people to?" he had screamed at one of Memphis' finest the night before this hot July afternoon.

"Sir, are you one of the family?"

"Yeah, yeah, umma brother. Where'd you takem?"

"Mister, come sit down in the car with me pleasuh; this might be a blow toya."

And then he knew.

"Sir, there just whadn't nobody to take nowhere. They just… um… very sorry sir. Do you know how many people were in the truck? We can't even tell that. They're all just kinda melted together."

"You have a lotta class, you know that?"

"My job is not to have class sir; my job is to do my job. Now, how many people were in the truck, and who was your sister?"

"There was one person and two dogs in that truck."

"Dogs?"

"Yeah, the two-legged kind. The person was Siedah Jackson, an engineer from New Orleans. Somebody I let ... slip through my fingers. `I think it's funny, funny, funny how time just slips away.'"

"Are you ok? Why are you singin? The other two?"

"I don't know their names ... don't know if they had names. Swamp creatures they don't give names to, just political posts. Anyway, they kidnapped my girlfriend when we were over in south Memphis digging... er... diggin some sounds at the CLUB IMPRESSIONS on Elvis Presley. And I guess she must have grabbed the wheel or kicked the driver in the nuts or something, cause here's this burnin wreck with the charred bones. Does that complete 'your job'?"

"Any idea why they woulda wanted to kidnap this Miss Jackson?"

" ... ah, well officer, if you coulda seen this woman in an aerobics suit ..."

* * *

But where had the load they'd been carrying gone to? Where was that hump under the sheet that Dennis had seen? For all he knew, Dennis could have been hallucinating. Poor Dennis. The medical doctors, those rich incompetents masquerading as humanitarians, said that he had a severe concussion and wanted to know who carried his insurance. He'd be in the hospital a while. The deal had gone sour for him too. And Siedah ...

"Shit is just all outta whack sometimes. We do stuff in search of things we think make life worth living: money and all it can buy, notoriety, reputation. We go thousands of miles from home thinking that just around the corner there's got to be a place where stuff makes sense. We do stuff that my grandmother would have laughed at. She woulda said `Boy, at home I can look out for you, do things for you. You can make a way right here at home. When you far away from me, I can't do nothin for you but pray.'

"For the sake of postcontemporary notions of success, we transgress against everything love and family are supposed to be about, and then expect everything to come out the same way it did before our time, a period we know nothing about cause we'd rather watch *The Wheel of Fortune* than struggle through a history book by Van Sertima or C. Williams, and a period which whadn't necessarily better—but we know the present ain't workin out. So we just try to get out of it. Fans run to the past; Afros—especially the white ones—flee for the future. Granma would never have thought of leaving home looking for something, cause she woulda known that long-distance-love is too hard on love. She knew you got a few little years here, where you gon struggle and groan anyway, and you may as well be in the vicinity of ready-made-love while you tryin to make a buck.

"Ha! Well, at least I wasn't damn fool enough to go north. Ha! Them Southern niggers always come draggin home in the end realizin that they can't do without that home they love and hate so intensely at the same time. It's home."

People jumped off Zip's side of the sidewalk, ducked into alleys until he passed, stood in the downtown lunchhour traffic rather than come in contact with yet another urban lunatic, this one in muddied bluesatin jumpsuit with nappy, bloodied hair yet, screaming out loud to himself.

"And what am I ramblin about here? What am I tryin to say? It's that I still believe anything is better than standin still. The alternative to not tryin is to do nothing, become a FAN, somebody who does nothing so he won't have to face failure, who only stands by and criticizes others who fail in their attempts at success in this thing we call LIFE. So I tried and I was groovin, but never as well as when I found Si, right here in this life, putting her tongue in my ear and teachin me the code of love, code of survival. And to run so far to get away from shit that I thought was holdin me down, love being onea those things, only to be missing it so dearly right here, right now, downtown on the mall ..."

Zip made the left at the deli onto Front. He could see Siedah's apt. window from there. In it hung her charm that she took with her everywhere she went: a 3" x 3" x 3" golden triangle, a pyramid, on a golden chain, that caught the glint of the purple sun falling slowly, slowly into the Mississippi.

* * *

For the next 24 hours, he neither ate nor drank nor slept, but wrote like a wild man on her giant, rented, mahogany desk, trying to put into words the way things are, and the way things would be; fictionalize the whole account to make it believable, send it to Professor Ward to see if he could market it; if it hit, it'd be the last honest thing he'd ever write, because fame was both nectar and poison. Just stick it all in the mail post-marked for New Orleans, and then go on his hands and knees, as fast as the Dog would carry him, back to Atlanta and Mr. Hugh … and Peggy.

At sunset, the doorbell rang.

* * *

"BABYBABYBABY! came out all muffled and slobbery because he couldn't take his tongue out of Siedah's mouth long enough to speak clearly. In the flesh, there she was, resurrected, a Phoenix, all in purple and alive and beautiful. And the subject of the treasure didn't come up again until the sweat and love had evaporated from the desk, and Zip and Si lay nude on the floor in the glow of the river landing lights.

* * *

" … and so I rolled the head down the green and pushed it down a slope deep into the woodscovered it with as many sticks and branches as I could, and passed out.

"Zip, it wasn't like we thought. Those slaves didn't smelt any gold and pour it into the brass mold to form the head. That head was always already formed! The brass must have been hammered around it to protect it before it was buried. It musta come from somewhere in West Africa cause I could see Youraban religious symbols etched into the soft gold as I was rolling it into the woods. But the head seems to be of Khmtic-Kushite stock, so why would it have Vodoun inscriptions set in circles from the land of the Yorubas and the mass-murdered Ibos?

"Zip you've never seen anything so beautiful in your life. I mean, nothing can compare, not even the Temples at Karnak and Luxor, or the Taj Mahal, or Steiglitz's photo of the then-new Brooklyn Bridge at night, or Stella's abstract painting of the same bridge, or that new mile-tall IBM Tower in New York, or that look in Billy Dee's eyes in the club scene of *Lady Sings the Blues*, or that new, nude bust of Rhianna in the National African Art Museum of the Smithsonian, or *1999*, or—"

"—ok, I get the idea. This is one hell of a head. Jez, it must be something to impress you, the person that's seen everything and done everything with the person who invented the thing. You usually come on so cool."

"Oh honey! That 8' x 8' head is made of the purest gold that was mined—

wherever it was mined. Weren't King Solomon's mines in W. Africa? Anyway, around the 1-foot circumference eyes are 100 of the finest diamonds, each one an inch in diameter. In the right nostril of the nose, a gigantic turquoise stone that must be as large as my head. And the eyes themselves Zip! I don't know what they are. Somebody painted them over with gold gilt.

And around the edges of the jaws where they meet the sculpted braids, there were still traces of black and green oil-based paint that must have been used to frame and set-off the jaws, cheekbones, and eyes. So I'm only guessing that the brass must have been hammered-out and shaped around the head to prevent further damage, but the moisture from the ground got to the head and corroded the paint and darkened the gold. And I can't tell you how old it is, but for sure it's at least 2500 years before Christ or Rome or Greece even, and it's crafted more finely than anything from those recent periods. When you see it—I don't know why—you have to fall on your knees."

"Maybe it makes us remember what we were once before we fell and hit our heads. Maybe it brings our heads and our hearts back to ourselves. You know how art works wonders even when literalists don't want it to," said Zip.

"Yeah. But Zip, three other things: first, when I rolled it into the woods I could hear something deep inside of it moving, and it sounded like something solid and heavy. And the base of the neck was jagged, not smooth, like it had been separated from something."

"God Siedah, you don't think ... what was the last thing?"

"Chiseled into the jagged grooves was an inscription in what I took to be Merotic scriptographs."

"Goddam Siedah, how do you know all this incredible shit? You're an engineer!"

"Boy, you not the only one who reads. You think you the only one who knows what time it is?"

"Well ... and what did the inscription say?"

Siedah strolled 150 pounds of brown blessing to the window, crossed her arms in front of her nipples, already hardening again, and spoke to the wet night air, as the river sloshed on the stones, and then she turned and faced southeast.

"From the little Merotic script I can still remember from that summer I spent at the ASCAC Conference in Chicago, I think it says something like,

'Omitunde—', er, I mean:

**"AS WATER, OUR CHILDREN ALWAYS RETURN!/
COME BACK TO KHMT./
COME BACK TO THE BLACK LAND./
SEE THE CRADLE CITY/
THE PLACE WHERE YOU CAME INTO BEING./
KISS THE GROUND AT THE GREAT GATE/
AND BE ALWAYS AMONG FRIENDS."**

Zip, hardening again too, looking at Siedah as she slowly turned and walked toward him, tears in his eyes, raised himself up from the floor where he had been sitting, pressed his knees to the floor, leaned back on his arms, and lowered his head toward Siedah as her hips enveloped him.

* * *

"So it was just a goddamed miracle that I got thrown clear, out onto the green behind the head. Oh Zippy, you're alive!"

"Baby, I thought you was gone for sure too, and now here we are in the afterglow. Ha! Wait til you see the shit I wrote about us. You'll split! I was driving all over the city, runnin pickups off the street, and I heard on the ZXX+'s radio that something had blown up in the park. I knew it had to be your volatile ass. Look, I even wrote a bad piece of confessional poetry and stuck it in the novel:

"They write poems about the night.
They speak of night life
and dancing and love and sex and the first rays of dawn.

Tomorrow night I will speak your virtues and faults to one
who does not deserve to hear the sound.
And forever I will tell to someone,
as we clutch tightly on the dance floor,
our whole story,
tell it to someone who will not understand a thing about us.
And forever I will raise and rub and clutch and kiss,

and at the end scream your name
in cotton sheets where your silken memory should never be.

The night.

They write poems about the night.
They speak of night life:
Dancing and love and sex and the first rays of dawn."

"Damn, it's beautiful, but you didn't even wait for my ashes to get cold before you're out starting other fires trying to forget me. Where's Dennis?"

"Still in the hospital. He got jammed on the head by the same boys you turned into crap casserole. They moved him out of intensive care though. He's gon be fine. He'll be even finer when I tell him we got the head back."

"Zip, it may not even be there now. How long was I out for? When I came to, there was birddo all over me, and I just threw some more stuff on top of the head, traded a guy in the Goodwill store a gold band for some shoes and a leotard and thumbed my way down here. You had to be here. You just had to. But I don't know if the head's still there, and even if it is, we got ourselves a bigger problem."

"What are you talking about?"

"Zip, have you thought about how that head was made?"

"Well, those slaves, my relatives helped to make it goddamit."

"No, I don't mean how it was formed or painted or buried or anything; I mean how it was *gotten* by Winchester."

"Well, he... what do you mean?"

"Zip, are you gon be able to enjoy spending money, having money made at the cost of the lives of your own relatives and so many other blacks when Winchester was implementing his Grand Design for the Illusion of Dixie? You know, *he* may have had added to that head some gold or some diamonds. The southerners also paid him in precious metals and precious stones to kill. According to Mrs. Jones, he wouldn't take Confederate currency. And he used that wealth to buy his 6—your relatives—and no telling how many other Africans, and to finance his voyage to West Africa in the first place. I mean, Zip, it's as bloody as bloodmoney can get."

"I... I hadn't thought—"

"You hadn't thought?! When I was out I dreamed somea the wildest dreams. I mean, they were from the right side of the brain. Bizarre, but so

... real. All these black relatives of yours kept coming to me telling me the tragedy that was their lives here in the States. They were in this long line that was like in chronological order. Each generation following the next, and it just went on and on. And, finally, at the end of this line was Menes"

"So he cut line, and in the wrong place! How typical of my family."

"Shut up fool. This is serious. Anyway, his story ended with the head. How the gold and diamonds were their gold and diamonds more than it could ever have been Winchester's. That his brothers and nephews found out about the head while Winchester was away, and how they dug it and Menes up and put the head under him and buried him back on top of it. And how there was more suffering than gold packed into that bejeweled head, and so your relatives couldn't use it... wouldn't use it. How that golden head belonged with those who had made it. And that that's who ought to have it. Then you know what he did?"

"What?"

"He farted and patted me on the ass and faded out."

"Yep. My ancestor all right. Well, whata you wanna do?"

"I don't know. It was your folks."

"The money we'll get from that head is as much yours and Dennis' as it is mine and Menes.'"

"Well, so whata you wanna do baby?"

"Damn, it sure is blood money like all money but even worse. I ... I just don't know; first we check out the head. Then, if it's still there, we go to Budget and rent a truck with a covered storage area and a forklift gate. If it's not there, all our moral problems are solved, and we can get on with our future. We'll know what time it is. If it's there, well, then, the responsibility is on my head, er, so to speak. Shit, I don't know. If we could just learn to be more bloodthirsty and moneyhungry, we'd have a lot more houses in the suburbs I'll tell you that."

"Yeah, but, y'know, then we wouldn't be us."

Siedah curled her long arm around Zip's naked chest and held him tight.

"Yeah, but, you know Si, I don't even know if anybody would notice."

* * *

As he lay there in the diffused and reflected neonlight from the River landing, Zip's mind raced over so many things. At least the world was back on its axis again now, with Siedah snuggled close to his chest, one of her long legs over his thigh and curled under his calf.

Had his love for Siedah proven that money was not the most important thing in a world that runs on money? That love overshadowed and dispelled everything negative, like with the parents who still love their doomed children and who gon have more in the midst of New Orleans' most crime ridden project? Did love dispel all that sorrow? Was love a drug that made us forget that we had soberly stumbled into a square sphere?

And had his pilgrimage proved that love came when it wanted to come, where it wanted to come, and how it wanted to come? That it was just as likely to grab you by your naked butt in your own bathtub in Memphis as it was likely to fall from a palm tree in some exotic place that you see in the TV commercials?

Had all his searching and singing and yearning uncovered, through total ignorant chance, a white boy with as much sense of humanness as he? A man who could show him that you have to fight to be successful at being human. A man who woke up long before he was born to know that you live not only for yourself right now but for those you want to love later. Did true, human love not only come in all colors but also with sweat stains under its frayed jacket and scarred Adidas that couldn't even be given to Goodwill? Could such an other-worldly thing be possible?

Was the confident self who crooned all that pop music when he was on stage in Atlanta the same as the insecure and disgruntled self who moaned the blues like a Muddy Waters clone in his bedroom mirror at night? Did song work for Afros the same way sand worked for micro-chips: worthless by itself but able to hold whole libraries of importance once it was turned into a refined version of itself? Could the song reconstruct and revitalize an existence if one found the secret to turning the song back onto itself and erasing existence to supplant it with a secret, liveable illusion?

Could historical occurrences started millennia ago really symbiotically intertwine and rebound into real time, bringing with them reclaimable mysteries, retrievable history, reluctant confessions, redeemable remnants, redoubtable relationships, recalcitrant renegades, relativistic, redeemable wealth, and respectable reasons to carry on in the current time frame of the here-and-now? Was the past really able to stick its nose into the present and teach you a lesson about being human for the future?

Could there exist a lover so filled with heat and seriousity, so evolved from the essences of everything that's essential, so built that she bumped you into feeling even when you were fighting not to feel, so cool that cool was not cool enough a word for her cool, wrapped up in wonderment and purple satin, moving like an angel on helium, so conversant with the ethereal side of what was up that she could make you laugh off cancer and make you know for sure what time it is? Could a lover like that be born in the Parish of New Orleans, or did you just dream her up, never wanting to awake?

If the love of money is the root of all bad roots, and some blood-money roots are worse than other bad roots, was it still possible to take that corrupted root and grow a rose? If the Big Clock goes tick-tock only when a token is dropped in, and you have to pay to play anyway or be stuck on a perpetual plane that leads only to the welfare and social services offices, why not groove with the gold no matter how its gotten? If the head were there, would he just go back and bury it with Menes and get on with the business of loving Siedah, singing, and living a life he wouldn't be ashamed of when all those helpful, hardened, strangers stood over his deathbed in some antiseptic hospital room?

WOULD HE REBURY THE HEAD?

* * *

Occasionally, Zip pondered these elastic, existential questions, as the Nigerian-rubbered whitewalls hummed beneath his customized Phantom Rolls Royce. Occasionally he murmured some phrases to Siedah, as he passed her yet another glass of Pouilly Fuisse `87 and for himself cracked yet another blue and white bottle of club soda, that perhaps love is more important than money in the washed out system under which he and she now prospered; that perhaps past people giving something in their presents made love possible for people far in the future.

Occasionally, he'd think on these difficult queries as he again howled when he looked over the eel-skin briefcase full of Dennis' cards with the 2-dimensional drawings and the postmarks from Rio. Rewriting the instructions for the proper directional placement of the head (sans the jewels) when he modemed messages to the Ethiopian State Museum at Addis Ababa, he'd occasionally slide his side up against Siedah's and try to intuit the answers from her force-field. Sometimes when he laughed about the exact replica of a Sparkling Inns three-bedroom LA condo he'd bought for his old phone-mates in Memphis, he'd close his eyes and meditate on how it was possible for any diverse and sacred human personalities to survive a corporate-clone system of degradation and insult.

Occasionally, when he thought of the one-inch equals one-foot version of the Temple of Abydos (Aabuju) he'd bought for his parents to live in, he'd reflect on the **kas** of Lester and Carrie and wonder how their evolution process had gotten speeded up and left all the other humans behind. Occasionally, when he received thank you notes from Soweto and Sugar Ditch where they'd sent half their shares, he'd lean back on the soft, Senegalese leather, tell Duffy to turn the Blu-ray low, and ask Si all the questions he'd now asked himself a thousand times. Cause, surely, if anybody had the answers to LIFE's questions, Siedah Jackson did.

He asked her all these questions, and she the same things of him, as the Rolls hummed through Beverly and Hollywood Hills toward their state-of-the-art music studio or toward their Malibu beach-house with the DVD library of 50,000 titles.

Occasionally they asked each other all these things.

But only occasionally.

Also Available from UNO Press:

William Christenberry: Art & Family by J. Richard Gruber (2000)

The El Cholo Feeling Passes by Fredrick Barton (2003)

A House Divided by Fredrick Barton (2003)

Coming Out the Door for the Ninth Ward edited by Rachel Breunlin from The Neighborhood Story Project series (2006)

The Change Cycle Handbook by Will Lannes (2008)

Cornerstones: Celebrating the Everyday Monuments & Gathering Places of New Orleans edited by Rachel Breunlin, from The Neighborhood Story Project series (2008)

A Gallery of Ghosts by John Gery (2008)

Hearing Your Story: Songs of History and Life for Sand Roses by Nabile Farès, translated by Peter Thompson, from The Engaged Writers Series (2008)

The Imagist Poem: Modern Poetry in Miniature edited by William Pratt, from The Ezra Pound Center for Literature series (2008)

The Katrina Papers: A Journal of Trauma and Recovery by Jerry W. Ward, Jr., from The Engaged Writers Series (2008)

On Higher Ground: The University of New Orleans at Fifty by Dr. Robert Dupont (2008)

Us Four Plus Four: Eight Russian Poets Conversing translated by Don Mager (2008)

Voices Rising: Stories from the Katrina Narrative Project edited by Rebeca Antoine (2008)

Gravestones (Lápidas) by Antonio Gamoneda, translated by Donald Wellman, from The Engaged Writers Series (2009)

The House of Dance and Feathers: A Museum by Ronald W. Lewis by Rachel Breunlin & Ronald W. Lewis, from The Neighborhood Story Project series (2009)

I hope it's not over, and good-by: Selected Poems of Everette Maddox by Everette Maddox (2009)

Portraits: Photographs in New Orleans 1998-2009 by Jonathan Traviesa (2009)

Theoretical Killings: Essays & Accidents by Steven Church (2009)

Voices Rising II: More Stories from the Katrina Narrative Project edited by Rebeca Antoine (2010)

Rowing to Sweden: Essays on Faith, Love, Politics, and Movies by Fredrick Barton (2010)

Dogs in My Life: The New Orleans Photographs of John Tibule Mendes (2010)

Understanding the Music Business: A Comprehensive View edited by Harmon Greenblatt & Irwin Steinberg (2010)

The Fox's Window by Naoko Awa, translated by Toshiya Kamei (2010)

A Passenger from the West by Nabile Farès, translated by Peter Thompson, from The Engaged Writers Series (2010)

The Schüssel Era in Austria: Contemporary Austrian Studies, Volume 18 edited by Günter Bischof & Fritz Plasser (2010)

The Gravedigger by Rob Magnuson Smith (2010)

Everybody Knows What Time It Is by Reginald Martin (2010)

mN
nw
o-